Anna H. Drury

The Brothers

Vol. 2

SALZWASSER
VERLAG

Anna H. Drury

The Brothers

Vol. 2

Reprint of the original, first published in 1865.

1st Edition 2022 | ISBN: 978-3-75258-983-2

Verlag (Publisher): Salzwasser Verlag GmbH, Zeilweg 44, 60439 Frankfurt, Deutschland
Vertretungsberechtigt (Authorized to represent): E. Roepke, Zeilweg 44, 60439 Frankfurt, Deutschland
Druck (Print): Books on Demand GmbH, In de Tarpen 42, 22848 Norderstedt, Deutschland

THE BROTHERS

A Novel.

BY

ANNA H. DRURY,

AUTHOR OF "DEEP WATERS," "MISREPRESENTATION," ETC.

IN TWO VOLUMES.

VOL. II.

LONDON:

CHAPMAN AND HALL, 193, PICCADILLY.

1865.

CONTENTS OF VOL. II.

THE BROTHERS.

CHAPTER I.

HOW ROLAND DID WHAT ENGLAND EXPECTED.

SEPTEMBER came and went, and the partridges received their due attention, and October had brought the same respectful notice on the pheasants, when Roland bade adieu to his home, and went up to town to prepare for his examination. Gervase Wray was in London now, and they were to be together for the present, while the candidate for official honours was studying that formidable Modern History, which appalled him the more he looked at it. What to him were the Pragmatic Sanction, or the Thirty Years' War, that he must give them the time and attention which he could devote so much more agreeably, if not profitably, elsewhere? How maddening it was to be told by those who had *not* passed, that you never, by any chance, were asked questions on the subjects you got up best—that the examiners were always hunting out old things from Annual Registers, that nobody but the Annual Registrar, whoever he might be, ever thought worth remembering—and that the marks you got did not depend on your real capacity (this seemed the crowning aggravation of all), but on the peculiar notions of your judge on sundry points—notions which you had no possibility of getting at beforehand. Over and over again he despaired of success in learning and remembering everything that had ever happened in the world; and as often, after some tremendous walk, returned to the undertaking in perfect good faith, that as it was expected of him, he must somehow manage to do it. He was working as he had never worked in his life, for it was with a glad hope before him; and if Marion's eyes would sometimes look out of his page rather too brightly for serious reading, they shone no less through the clouds of disgust and weariness, to cheer him on with the vision of a happy future, when history and geography might be as if they had never been.

He had kept his resolution bravely, and though he had often been at the Vicarage, and a friendly intercourse had been carefully maintained between the houses, he had never told his love to Marion in words. If his looks and manner betrayed it, so much the better; he was not going to act a part to please anybody, and nobody thought of expecting that he should. They met, not so often as he could have wished, but often enough to make them both very happy, and cause the blank of his departure to be sensibly felt. She understood why he was going, and what he hoped for, and she encouraged him by all the means in her power; but she missed him grievously, and thought the time would never come to an end. Fortunately, perhaps, that autumn was a sickly one in Stourbrooke, and there was so much illness and distress among the villagers, that even Mrs. Brudenell's care for her niece's newly recovered strength gave way before the urgencies of duty, and Marion took her first lesson in parochial usefulness among the beds of the sick and dying. There was work enough to employ every available hand, and she made a much more rapid progress under the pressure of necessity, than if there had been time for her to think whether she were doing everything well or badly. Her health improved instead of suffering from the unwonted exertion; her colour and bloom returned as she accompanied her aunt, in the darkening afternoons, to outlying cottages, where a nurse could not be had for love or money, and where, while Mrs. Brudenell attended to the invalids, she put her hand to all manner of domestic tasks—the more readily for her continental training. Many a little service was she enabled to render, from having been allowed, during her late sojourn at her *pension*, to beguile some of the hours in helping the good old *bonne*:—accomplishments of which Mr. Saville had more than once reaped the benefit, though without investigating their origin. It charmed Mrs. Brudenell to find her niece so ready with her hands; and though their ideas on sick cookery differed in some essentials, she could bear to be opposed by Marion, if by nobody else, and was brought to admit that some of the *bonne's* recipes were not without merit, though she believed a good sensible mutton-chop was worth them all.

On these expeditions they constantly met Cecil Percival, who gave himself no rest night or day. It did not quite agree with him as with Miss Egerton; for he was one who needed rest, and looked as if he were burnt up with fever; but no persuasion would make him call in Dr. Wartop, and the latter was too full of work to press his services. The state of the place delayed the proposed arrangements at the White House. Not even Stella's authority could have made Mrs. Porchester risk herself where there was danger of infection; and Stella herself was daunted by the accounts she heard. So they agreed, for once, on paying visits in the interval, and deferring their final move till the epidemic was past.

Harcourt gave liberally, paid all expenses required of him, refused nothing in the way of repairs, drainage, and other sanitary measures, and was generous in remission of rent where payment was impossible. But he avoided the dying, and seemed painfully depressed when any such cases were forced on his notice. His housekeeper told Mrs. Brudenell he was falling into his gloomy habits again, and shutting himself up in his private apartments; and she did think it so bad for so young a gentleman, she hoped the ladies would persuade him out of it. And as nothing had ever passed, since his rejection, to make Marion uncomfortable in his presence, beyond the regret of having given him pain, he was asked to the Vicarage, and pressed to come often, and so kindly received when he did come, that he came nearly every day.

They thought no harm, for the Vicar and his wife believed his offer had only originated in honourable generosity, and, while they respected him for it, had no idea his heart had been touched; and if Marion judged otherwise, she imagined him perfectly cured. She knew he had been the first to urge his cousin to settle near him, and that, she said to herself, he never would have done, had he meant to trifle with her regard. His coming in this way was just what she could have wished, enabling her to treat him, without fear of misconstruction, as so generous a friend deserved. And so he saw her daily, and under all circumstances; and she lost all fear and restraint in his presence, and talked to him freely, and listened to him with interest, as a brother—dear for his own sake, dearer still for Roland's. And the oftener they met, the more plainly he discovered that she was becoming dearer to him than life, than brotherhood, than honour. He could not love a little—in his nature a sentiment became a passion; and passion, where the soul has virtually cast off the only government that can hold it back, or keep it down, too surely becomes master of all. He shuddered as he read his own heart; he would hurry home after a cheerful half-hour, sometimes the most they could spare him, to stifle thought by occupation, going over the White House, lavishing expense upon Stella's favourite improvements, or writing encouraging letters to Roland, with offers of supplies—as if thereby to atone to both. Roland, however, was in a very economical mood at present; would only accept a moderate allowance, declined horse or servant, and resisted all temptations to needless expenditure. He could be firm, too, when his mettle was roused; and from the day that Harcourt sold the greys, he had resolved to cost him as little as he could help. If he sometimes sighed, on a warm, foggy morning, to think what a hunting day it must be in the country, his regret did not damp his industry, which, as the time drew near, became more ambitious than ever. He refused all invitations, resisted seductive play-bills and opera-tickets, and lived in an atmosphere of Modern History, that drove Gervase Wray nearly wild. He was thankful when a pressing invitation to meet Mrs. Porchester at the house of a mutual friend, gave him a fair excuse for leaving the student to fight his battles alone, as even his tried good humour gave way beneath the infliction of being pelted with miscellaneous historical questions at every meal. He went to meet Mrs. Porchester, and take her orders for the move to the White House, and Roland, to the great joy of his half-maddened tutor, went up for his examination, and, in due course, passed—a feat which amazed himself, and excited some disgust in those he had beaten, who murmured at the injustice of being pitted against Oxford men. By this great victory, he was admitted to the dignity of a clerk in her Majesty's —— Office, with a salary, about two-thirds less than what he spent as pocket-money, and the prospect of rising by degrees for the remainder of his days. Sir Perkin, the head of that department, to whom he announced his success, wished him joy, told him his fortune was made, invited him to dinner, and promised him early leave of absence to go down and see his brother. The sound of leave of absence had an official ring about it that charmed Roland's ears, accustomed as he was to go and come as he pleased, without any leave but his own; and he trod the pavement, after quitting the presence, with a consciousness of having done what England expected him to do, and a strong sense of what she might be expected to do for him in return.

He was dressing in haste for Sir Perkin's dinner-party, when Wray's servant came in to announce that a Frenchman, giving the name of Auguste, had called several times to see his master, and would Mr. Clarendon be so good as to tell him when he might be expected to return?"

"Auguste? Ask him if he was Mr. Saville's valet at Baden. What on earth can have brought him here?" he said to himself, as he went on brushing vigorously at his luxuriant locks. "Ah! come in, Auguste! Glad to see you, though in this darkness it sounds rather like an empty compliment. Bring in another candle, Timbs, and stick it into Mr. Wray's account. Not exactly the skies of Baden or Switzerland, Auguste? I thought you were basking in the sunshine of Rome all this time."

"Sare, I did go to Rome; Monsieur Wray he was so kind to recommend me to one gentleman, and I did go wiz him, but he was not the gentleman I was used to serve—he did not know how to treat his valet-de-chambre as I had been treated, and I left him, and came to London to make my fortune, sare, you know. It is not to be made by standing still in ze fog—everyzing in London so dear, so dear!"—he held up both his hands—"you pay for ze air you breathe, and you get no air but coal smoke. Ah! what a climate! Monsieur Wray, will he soon be in town again?"

"I expect him any day; he is enjoying

himself in the country, and if he is wise he will stay there, where I should be, but for my duty. It is new for me to be in London in the hunting season, Auguste," he went on, as he put the finishing touches to his toilet, "but you must know I am now a Government official, a servant of her Majesty's. I have just passed, and a very stiff examination too," dwelling on the phrase with great relish. "We are rather particular now about the kind of men we put into office, and a certain amount of talent and knowledge is required, which all men have not the means of possessing. Even *I* had to buckle to, I can tell you; and Mr. Wray had enough of it, poor man, and was glad to get out of hearing. You see, I want to make my fortune as well as you, so I am working hard for it. Halloa! it is time I was off. Run for a cab, Timbs, there's a good fellow; I must not go in to dinner smelling of this fog. What can I do for you, Auguste? It is a bad business for you to be out of place."

"If you could recommend me to any gentleman who wanted a first-rate valet, or any family who required a confidential man-servant to go abroad, Mr. Roland. Zere is my address, my *logement* at present. Ah! such a *logement* for such a price! Zey are zieves, ze London *proprietaires*, and zer wives are worse.

Zey take all your money, and your coals, and your *café*, and your little property, and zey abuse you to your face. Ah!"

"Then if I hear of anything I may let you know. All right; help me on with that great-coat—thank you. If I were a rich man, I would engage you myself."

"Ah, if I could meet with one master like you, M. Roland, or *M. votre frère*, I would die content. Can you tell me, sare, any news of Mademoiselle? She is not married yet—no?"

"Not that I am aware of," said Roland, smoothing his hat.

"Ah no—not till ze *deuil* is over, assuredly. But after zat, it will be soon, hein?"

"That is more than I can tell you, Auguste. "Have you any special interest in the matter?"

The man's small black eyes twinkled eagerly. "Interest, yes—Mademoiselle is just—she is true—she is generous—she will do what is right when she is rich. I have no fear."

"Nor I, but I doubt her being rich in a hurry—if you are talking of Miss Egerton?"

"Ah, sare, I understand—she has had great wrong too. I know, I know"—striking his breast, and shaking his head; "but it is not for me to speak of her affairs. When she is rich, she will remember me. And Mademoiselle *votre cousine, la plus belle des belles*, as poor Monsieur called her, she is well?"

"I hope so. Mr. Wray is gone to meet her, and my aunt, and arrange about their coming to live near us in the country. Now really, my good fellow, I must go, or I shall be late, and to be too late at the house of the Head of my Department, would indeed be a breach of manners. Come and see me to-morrow morning if you like, and we will see what can be done for you.—What did he mean by talking of Marion's marriage, and of what she would do when she grew rich, I wonder?" thought he, as he drove along. "Like the impudence of those foreign flunkeys, to talk about her at all. Heigh-ho! How long shall I be climbing to the top of this official tree? It seems a year since I saw her, and I am still only scrambling at the lower branches. How I wish I knew what she is doing at this moment!"

The party was a well-selected one, and Roland received a gratifying welcome. His mother's kinsman, General Alexander, was one of the guests, as well as his daughter, a young widow lady, whom Roland had not seen since he was a schoolboy, but who at once claimed his acquaintance, and contrived to sit next to him at dinner. His left-hand neighbour was a rather shy young maiden, making her first appearance in public, and decidedly preferring *her* left-hand supporter, whom she knew well, to the tall cavalier she had never met before; so he had less scruple in allowing Mrs. Lyndsay to absorb his attention. She had travelled, and seen a great deal of society, and knew something about everybody; and a more agreeable companion at a dinner-table could not well have been found, especially as she seemed determined he should be agreeable too. Everybody knows how delightful that person is who draws you skilfully out, and causes you to appear to advantage—and Mrs. Lyndsay was known in the world as a most delightful woman.

She had been abroad the greater part of the year, intending to winter in Rome, but had been recalled from the latter place by her father's state of health. He had complained of loneliness, and she had come back to cheer his winter evenings.

"No persuasion will make him give up office, though I know it will end in his breaking down altogether, so all I can do is to help the harness to sit as lightly as possible. If I had my own way, I would take it off altogether."

"I am very glad you have not. Here am

I, just beginning to climb, and wanting every friendly hand I can lay hold of, and you are trying to rob me of my chief supports. The country cannot spare General Alexander, and the country, you know, is above everything."

"Oh yes, we know all about that; your country means your salaries, and so long as those are regularly paid, you care for little else. I have not congratulated you yet on your blushing honours. I hope to live to see you Secretary of State, and as hard to persuade into a holiday as you are now eager to get it. And when may I congratulate you on another score?"

"On what?" asked he, with an unreasonable idea that she might have heard of his attachment.

"On your brother's engagement; or is it still to be kept a secret? I heard it talked of in Rome as a settled thing."

"The Romans are wiser than I, then. Who may the lady be? for I know he has been given to a great many."

"Of course he has; he must pay the penalty of being so hard to please. Any conscientious person in his place would have married long ago. We were all certain, at one time, that Stella Porchester would conquer the obdurate heart, but she has so many admirers, I suppose she has no leisure for fixing one."

"She is coming to live close to us," began Roland, perplexed by these remarks; "my aunt has taken a house of Harcourt's, and we expect them to take possession by Christmas."

"Ah, indeed! you surprise me. And the wedding? Come, with kith and kin you need not be so extremely close. You have been studying official reticence so perseveringly, that you cannot shake it off in social intercourse."

"I am not close, but dull, I am afraid, for I really do not know what you mean."

"I see you look mystified. Is it possible I am mistaken? I heard a most romantic story about the sudden death of a gentleman at Baden, who committed his daughter to your brother's care on his death-bed, and whom Harcourt was engaged to marry. I cannot recall the name at this moment, but my opposite neighbour will, for he knew something of him. Sir Henry!" addressing an elderly man at the other side of the table, decorated with one or two foreign orders, "what was the name of the gentleman we heard of, who died so suddenly at Baden-Baden this summer?"

"Do you mean poor George Saville?"

"Yes, thank you. Oh, and now I remember the facts; the young lady was his step-daughter, and as my story went, deeply attached to your brother; they had been wandering through Switzerland together. Come, you cannot plead ignorance now."

"Not as to the parties, certainly, for I was there at the time; but I believe you are mistaken as to the facts, as I rather think I should have known if such had been the case. Miss Egerton came over to England with our party, and is living with her uncle and aunt in our village, but beyond that, the romance is due to the imagination of your informant."

"Who could have told me? Stay, I will try and recollect. I heard it at Mrs. Marchmont's, in Rome, and I believe she said it came to her from the Sinclairs. Captain Sinclair afterwards talked about it himself. He was at Baden just after you all left, and met a friend of yours there, Gervase Wray. Everybody knows poor Gervase; I thought we should have seen him to-night."

"He is out of town. Pray go on."

"I have interested your incredulous ears, have I? Well, Captain Sinclair ought to know something of the business, for he hired Mr. Saville's valet on Gervase Wray's recommendation, and, ignominious as it may seem, I imagine the story came originally from him."

The room swam before Roland's eyes, the lights grew misty, and the voices sounded far off. In his confusion, he was awkward for the first time in his life, and broke a champagne glass over the delicate silk of his younger neighbour. The temporary disturbance thus caused, and the necessity of making atonement by apology and assiduous attention, fortunately prevented his betraying himself; and by the time he could turn again to Mrs. Lyndsay, she seemed to have forgotten their previous topic.

When the ladies left the dining-room, Roland placed himself near Sir Henry Mayne, and after the first glass of wine had been taken, brought on the subject of Mr. Saville. He found he had lighted on no sorrowing friend, like Mr. Brudenell, to whom every remembrance of that wasted life was a pain and a grief; Sir Henry knew Mr. Saville as others knew him—as the hero of many a good story, the point whereof lay in his accomplished roguery.

"Sinclair knows a good deal about him," he continued, peeling an orange; "do you know Sinclair? He is in Rome just now—we left him there. He took on Saville's valet, but found him too like his master to be a safe inmate. The fellow was always prying about, and getting at family secrets; and as he seemed as ready to impart information as to acquire it, this did not suit my friend at all. I only hope what he told was an invention of his own; those French rascals never stick to truth, if they can help it."

"Is that old Saville you are talking of?" asked a neighbour, who had not heard Roland's name; "was it true that he inveigled Harcourt Clarendon into promising to marry his step-daughter, by making him believe she was breaking her heart for him? It sounds almost too good a story to be true, but I was told it as a fact, and thought of writing to Clarendon to ask particulars."

"Here is his brother, who can give them, if you wish it," said Sir Henry, smiling blandly, as he quartered his orange; "let me introduce you—Mr. Graham—Mr. Roland Clarendon."

Mr. Graham looked a little confused, but apologised with a ready courtesy that silenced the angry words on Roland's lips. He was obliged to assume a good humour he was far from feeling, fingering nervously the stem of his wine-glass, and wishing the decorum of society permitted such a relief as it would be to send the contents into the speaker's face. Half conscious of having given offence, and willing to obliterate it if possible, Mr. Graham turned the conversation to safer topics; his cousin was Mr. Brudenell's friend, and though he was not often in that part of the world, and had never met Roland before, he knew enough of their common acquaintance to appear to know a great deal more.

"So Cecil Percival is doing duty in your place, I understand. Is he as strange as ever? He was the most extraordinary boy I ever saw, and by what I hear, he is unlike other people now."

"He is one of the best fellows breathing," said Roland.

"So my cousin said, and one of the most perverse. By the way, he is going to be married, is he not?"

"Upon my word, you seem to know a great deal more than I do; he may be, but I am not in the secret."

"Then Rumour is as bad as she is represented, for I heard it was to a beautiful relation of yours, who is about to be your neighbour."

"My aunt and cousin are coming to live near us—which of them is the lady in question?"

And Roland pinched the wine-glass harder still, and wished it were the decanter. Graham smiled, and shook his head. "I shall not commit myself again; only, if my news turns out to be truer than you think now, acquit me of being the gossip I appear. If I am misinformed, it is only representing both gentlemen as being more fortunate than they really are."

Sir Henry Mayne once more interposed, for he had been quietly noticing his young neighbour's face, and saw that it was time to change the subject; so he drew them both into discussion on sundry knotty points at that time engaging the attention of the sporting public, and kept it up till they rose from table.

Sir Perkin took hold of Roland's arm as they were leaving the dining-room. "Well, well, well? None the worse for cramming? None the wiser either, Percival would say. He has no faith in you prodigies of learning; declares one of my old clerks is worth a dozen of you. We mean to teach him he is wrong, do we not? We must march with the times, as I tell him, and if we are to have baths and wash-houses, and Saturday holidays, whereas in our young days people did without—so we must let the public work be done by young gentlemen who positively can spell their own names, and know that two and two make four. I am glad you got through—very glad. I spoke to my nephew to-day—he knows the chief of your room, and he will introduce you, and after that, you must get on by your own cleverness. But I say, my boy," in a lower key, "if you want to step into a good thing, stick to Alexander. He is a relation of yours, and was very fond of your mother; his private secretary is in bad health, and he likes a young one, and must have a gentleman. Charming woman his daughter; saw you getting on with her at dinner, you young fox; and you were quite right, for, between ourselves, she can get more out of the General than I can, or anybody else."

Roland was not in the most favourable mood for following this advice; irritated by all he had heard, and longing either to quarrel with somebody, or rush home to quarrel with himself, it was irksome to return to the bright drawing-room, and feel the necessity of having words and smiles ready at command. But fate and Mrs. Lyndsay were resolved he should not throw away all his opportunities; she soon regained possession of him, and having, by a coaxing gesture, brought her father near, contrived to make them better acquainted in a few minutes than they would otherwise have become in the course of months. The General decided that Clarendon was a fine, spirited youngster, very like his mother; and Roland, in no less complimentary style, admitted to himself, that if he must be a Private Secretary, he should not mind touching up the grammar of so jolly an old fellow as that. He quite looked upon the secretaryship as the due reward of his intense application and enormous knowledge; and felt it would be rather a favour to give his kinsman the preference. Notwithstanding this agreeable episode, however, he was impatient to depart; and when he had handed Mrs. Lyndsay into her carriage, slipped away, unobserved by any one but Richard Graham, who laughed as he wished him good night, and asked if he would take a bet on the accuracy of his fashionable intelligence. He had no idea how nettled Roland was already, or he would have let the subject alone; as it was, he received a very curt answer, and meeting Sir Henry Mayne soon afterwards, remarked that young Clarendon was a queer-tempered fellow—all the Clarendons were, he fancied. Indeed, Harcourt was more than queer—eccentric, at times, to an alarming degree;—would shut himself up for days together when a fit of moodiness was coming on.

"A very judicious measure," said Sir Henry, as he stepped into his carriage. "If everybody would do the same when their unwise fits came on, it would be better for all parties."

Roland, meanwhile, had thrown himself into a cab (economy being no object now his fortune was made), and was whirled to his lodgings at the full speed of the horse. The first thing he heard was that Gervase Wray had returned; and on ascending the stairs, he heard voices in his room. There was no mistaking the shrill broken English of Auguste, who having remained to gossip with Timbs, had caught his master on his arrival. The door being half open, and the man excited, Roland heard him distinctly as he came up.

"I tell you, sare, and I have told you before, he was one bad man—ver bad; he had no conscience—none! He rob you—he rob me—he rob ze small boy in ze street, if he have one sou to take hold off. He rob his wife, zat poor Madame, who give him all, and who died—ah! I know why; ze break her heart about him, and he no care; he eat, drink, sleep, all ze same. And he rob Mademoiselle of her last franc if he could. I say, he rob *me*—*me*, who live with him so long; he take all my *épargnes*, le fruit *de tant de sueurs*—all I save; he tell me he give me high interest, just as he give Mademoiselle—bah! as well toss it out of zat window. And he know zis not last for ever, and so he want to make one good marriage for Mademoiselle, and a good home for him and for me. He tell me she marry one rich man, and pay me double for what I lend. And he die, and leave no word about me, and Mademoiselle know nozing, and I am robbed. You tell me, Mr. Wray, zat all be right, but it is all wrong, and before Mademoiselle marries, she must hear me, and she shall."

"Of whom are you speaking?" asked Roland, who had stood unobserved in the doorway during the rapid utterance of the last few sentences. Wray, who was reclining in an easy-chair by the table, near which Auguste was gesticulating, occasionally thumping it with his flat hand, rose with alacrity to bid his friend welcome, giving him to understand by shrug and smile how bored he was by all this clamour.

"I am sure, Clarendon," he said, pointedly, "you will agree with me, that if there is any claim on Mr. Saville's estate, it would be much better to lay it quietly before his brother, and see what he will do, than to mix up Miss Egerton's name in an affair with which she can have no concern."

Not even his love for Marion could make Roland prudent at that moment. His temper had been too much ruffled already to tolerate that such lips should make free with that name; and regardless of Wray's hint, he turned fiercely round on the excited valet.

"I can only tell M. Auguste—and I advise him to attend seriously to what I say—that if I find him introducing that lady's name again into any story he may be inclined to repeat, or any complaint he has to lay against his late master, I shall take upon myself to make him repent it. He has talked a great deal too much already, and done quite enough mischief; and I warn him now, once for all, that Miss Egerton is not to be annoyed by his applications, or insulted by his conjectures and remarks. You understand plain English, M. Auguste?"

"Ah, sare, I understand *yours;* I have often understood you. You had a language of your own, zat a shild might soon learn. You did teach on ze palm of my hand, as if I was deaf-mute, yes—and so I was, but not blind. No, sare, no. I did wish you *bonheur*, but——" And he shrugged his shoulders, and raised the teachable palms he spoke of, in an indescribable attitude of regret at the ruthlessness of destiny; then moved to the door. Wray went with him into the passage, spoke a few conciliatory words, promised to let him hear the next day, and then came back to his friend.

"Rather suspicious, that last hint, Roland,"

he said, gaily. "I own I always thought you were mighty fond of the plausible rascal on the journey, though it was charitably supposed you were improving yourself in French. He is so proud of his English, however, I could not get him to speak his own language, and he has been going on with his 'bono Johnny' gibberish the last half-hour. I am so much obliged to you for stopping his tongue."

"I'll stop it effectually if he does not take my hint," said Roland. "Wray, I want to talk seriously to you."

"May I ask if it is on the Pragmatic Sanction?—for if it is——"

"Stuff! I have done with all that rubbish; this is something of real, vital importance. What can have led to such reports getting about as I have heard to-day?"

"What were they, in the first place?"

Roland detailed the remarks at Sir Perkin's table. Wray was silent for a short time; then leaning back in his chair, and striking the tips of his fingers lightly together, replied, "I believe I understand, if not the whole story, a great part of it. This babbling fellow may have fancied a great deal that never happened, but from what I saw, and what I know, I feel tolerably clear in the general facts. Mr. Saville, from whatever motive, let us hope from compunction, was as eager to secure a wealthy marriage for Miss Egerton as any fashionable mother could have been, and from the moment we all met, I know he kept his eye on Harcourt. He had shrewdness enough to see where the danger lay, and he made it his first business to lessen the influence of your beautiful cousin. Don't interrupt me; lookers-on see most of the game. He sounded me in his own charming way on your position, and your father's will; and after that, showed a marked preference for your brother. Indeed, he proved as much, by allowing him to pay for all her rides and excursions. You did not know that, I dare say, neither did she. Yes, he preferred Harcourt, certainly—the way of the world, you know—it does not follow that the young lady agreed with him. Whether he actually made a confidant of his valet, I cannot say, but the fellow seems to have guessed pretty nearly at the truth. The point where he shuffles and contradicts himself, is about a conversation he professes to have overheard between his master and Clarendon, which your brother says no one could have heard, the poor man spoke so low and indistinctly."

"Wray," said Roland, after a pause, in which he was revolving all he had heard, and trying to look the whole steadily in the face, "as a friend, caring for us all, what do you think about Stella and Harcourt? I have never yet had courage to press either of them on the subject, and sometimes I fancy one thing, and sometimes another."

"So do I," said Gervase Wray.

"You think Harcourt loves her?"

"I have thought so, but I have sometimes altered my opinion."

"She cares for him, surely?"

"I think she does; but, my dear fellow, it would be too presumptuous for you and me to pretend to fathom a woman's heart. I have sometimes doubted, and then—I will be as frank as you—I have been mad enough to wish."

"To wish what, old fellow? Anything in which I could help you?"

"No, Roland; you cannot give me fortune enough to make her care for *me*. She must be a rich man's wife, or she will be as miserable as she would make her husband."

"Poor old Gervase! Have you been her faithful slave so long, to feel for her like this? Has she any idea of it?"

"I believe she considers it a law of nature that every man should be her slave, or her tool. I am not sure which she is making

Percival, but if ever a man was stricken unto death, he is."

"Percival love Stella? But he always said he should not marry—he was in no position to think of domèstic happiness—it would take him from his work. Oh! it cannot be; he must see and know that Harcourt's claims are superior, and he is too conscientious to indulge in vain wishes and fancies. You know those clever young parsons get so much praise and respect from ladies, that they think nothing of it; and Cecil cares more to bring Stella to church, and to set her singing chants and hymns after his fashion, and not after the organist's, than he does for her beauty or her smiles. He wants to do her good, and she likes him for it, that is all. But I know what I shall do before I sleep; I shall write to old Oliver, and have it all out."

Roland's letter did not take very long; a letter seldom does, when the heart is full, and the hand is its faithful interpreter.

"MY DEAR HARCOURT,—I hope you received my few lines, announcing my success. It was a stiff examination, and I suppose I passed tolerably well, as Sir Perkin asked me to dinner to-day, and General Alexander was civil and good natured. His daughter, Florence Lyndsay, was there; nice and pleasant, and prettily dressed; no more like a widow than Stella, whom I hope never to see in that character, however becoming. Sir Perkin, by the way, put me up to a good thing; and if you hear of your little brother being appointed private secretary to a big-wig, and drawing a tip-top salary, you may perhaps admit for once, that the right man is in the right place. Our friend the Squire pooh-poohs these examinations, but I think they are the only way to secure good service, and keep out the idiots who can neither read nor spell.

"I am to be introduced to my chief to-morrow, and begin my duties at once. Sir Perkin has promised me an early leave of absence, as I am a little fagged, and shall be glad of a whiff of fresh air before settling down in earnest. I have no fear of not rising, as others have done, and the secretaryship seems pretty sure. So now I am fairly started, and can no longer refrain from entering on the subject nearest to my heart. It is no secret to you that I love Marion Egerton, for you knew it from the first. When you objected so strongly, you did not believe I was in earnest, and you disliked, very naturally, the idea of a connexion with poor old Saville. The more I hear of him, the more I feel you were right enough there; but the objection exists no longer, and to herself I defy the world to raise one. I knew I had no right to speak so long as I was idle, and I would not do so till I had given you notice. I want to be sure you will give me your hearty good will in the matter, and back me up, in case the old folks turn rusty. I shall speak for myself when I come down, but you might do something to smoothe my way. I rely on your kindness, as I have always had reason to do. Wray is just come back from a hard visit, where he has been talked to death by argumentative old ladies. He reports that Stella is determined to eat her Christmas dinner at the White House, so your people must look alive.

"That fellow Auguste has been pestering us to-night with his wants and complaints. I sent him about his business, which seems, on his own showing, to consist of meddling with other people's.

"Write by return of post, and tell me when you saw her last, and how the darling was looking. I only wish I could write to her myself, but I must be patient a little while longer. God bless you, my own dear brother.

"Yours ever,

"ROLAND CLARENDON."

CHAPTER II.

SCIENCE MADE EASY.

He had need of blessing, that brother well-beloved, when he had read that letter, and sat alone, considering how he should answer it.

He had foreseen that it would come to this; he had tried to reconcile himself to the thoughts of it; had walked though the rooms of the White House, conjuring up visions for his own illusion, with desperate resolves to believe in them, and finding them all dispelled by a single look from those eyes that were so unconscious of their own power. Never, since that day that she sat with him in his workroom, had he uttered a word to give her reason to believe he loved her; he had never renewed the subject with the Vicar, or touched on it with his wife; but this very reticence only served to fix it deeper in his own nature—a nature rarely hasty to receive an influence, and still more rarely disposed to lose it when once received. From interest and compassion, through regard and esteem, his sentiments towards Marion had gone on rapidly, silently, deepening in intensity, simply from passing through a heart unused to self-mastery on any higher principle than pride, or to be denied a single indulgence on which his will was set. And it had now become a passion which he had no strength to overcome—which the very thought of overcoming sent the proud blood surging through his veins, as though some audacious hand had been laid on his ancestral rights. So hotly did it surge, that he was obliged to sit some time, pressing his temples with his strong fingers, before he could safely rise from his chair. Silently he sat and thought through the long, lonely morning, brooding, in bitterness and sorrow of heart; for Roland, as we know, had been his angel, and he felt his love hung on that day's decision. And when at last he walked out in the clear, wintry air, to gain what relief action and exercise could give, that decision was not yet made, though the sorrow was rankling still.

He walked past the White House, turning his face away from it, and took the road that led to a hamlet which Marion regularly visited.

Perhaps he had an unacknowledged hope of meeting her; but if so, he was disappointed, for the visitor that afternoon was Cecil Percival, and at a turn of the road they met face to face. By a sudden impulse, such as drives men to measures they would have spurned had they been suggested, Harcourt resolved to consult this oracle, of whom no one could ever say that he had prophesied smooth things, or deceits, to high or low—to himself, least of all. He held out his hand more cordially than usual.

"I am glad to have met you, Percival; I am going to surprise you."

The curate stood still, breathless, but firm, as if expecting a blow. "How?" he asked, as he might have given the word "Fire!" to a file of executioners.

"By asking your advice."

"Indeed?" The word did not express much, but concealed a great deal.

"I have a point to decide between two men," Harcourt went on, looking, not at his adviser, but straight away at the distant landscape; "and the question I have to consult you on amounts to this. You teach the doctrine of self-abnegation (you see I have caught the correct word), of self-denial, of self, in short, put aside altogether, and on all occasions, in favour of everybody else. Is a man called upon by such a doctrine to give up to another the woman he loves?"

"What can have put it into your head to ask such a question of *me?*"

"Never mind that, if you can—if you dare answer it. I have not yet found the power, or the courage."

"I have always courage for the truth," said Percival, rather sternly; "it is easier to speak than it is to hear."

He stood thinking after saying this, and Harcourt did not disturb him.

"There are two ways of looking at your question," Cecil said, at last, "and I will state my opinion in very few words. If a man finds two people attached to each other, and because he forms a passion for the woman, endeavours to lure her from her plighted troth, that man is wrong—no matter how successful, or how true his love. But if he find himself opposed to a rival, whose best, or whose only right lies in his birth, or his position, or wealth, or his superior attractions, and the field is open to both—then I say, there is no duty that calls on him to give way. He may stand boldly forward in her sight and his, and win if he can, what he has lost."

The emotion with which he spoke would have betrayed to a less pre-occupied listener that more was meant than met the ear; but Harcourt was still looking far away, and only heeded the purport of his words.

"If I understand you," he said, presently, "you do not consider that of two men, with equal rights, the one ought to yield to the other."

"If both love equally, both have a right to win," returned Percival, "provided there be no prior claim on either side, in which case, a high-minded man must school himself, if he can, to bear the cross laid upon him. He can hardly bear a heavier."

"You think not? And you call such a thing a cross? I do not follow that phraseology. If it means something to be carried in a saintly manner, so as to draw admiration, and acquire merit, it cannot concern me, or— the parties I am speaking of. To them a wrong is a grievance to be righted, and a rival an obstacle to be put out of the way."

"Clarendon, in your very bitterness of tone, you betray the galling pressure on your shoulder. You have burdens to bear like others; be warned in time how you bear them. Carried in a higher strength than our own, they lift us upward; but rebelled against, thrown off, or misused, they become a weight that will crush us to powder."

"Well," said Harcourt, with a long, deep sigh, and attempt at a smile, "I may say, 'thou hast comforted me marvellous much.' It is not often I consult the oracle, either for myself or others, and it is a rare boon to get an answer that may be taken as you please. Thank you for listening to me; I will detain you no longer, for I know your time is precious."

"Will you permit me to detain you one moment in return?"

"Not if you are going to spoil your good service by any personal advice. I tell you honestly, I am in no state to bear it. You know yourself, that what may be very wholesome under one set of circumstances, may be equally dangerous under another."

"I never obtrude advice, Clarendon, and I should hardly begin now with you. If what I have to say concerns you, it equally concerns myself. I wish to ask you a serious question, and to make sure before I ask it that you will not consider it an offence."

"I can promise nothing; but if I do, it will not much matter, I suppose. I cannot call you out, and you would be a match for me in most things; at least, you would have been formerly. You have grown much thinner, Percival. Do you starve yourself, or what is the reason?"

"Thinner, am I?" He looked at his hands as if the idea were quite new. "Nonsense! I am as strong as a horse. A man does not live longer, or work better, for being like your sleek carriage-horses. I live only too well—too luxuriously. Clarendon, I must ask the question at once, or my nerve may fail. Are you engaged to your cousin?"

Harcourt stared at him in amazement at the unexpected query.

"Certainly not. Why do you ask me?"

"Is there any probability that you will be? Is her affection yours?"

"Upon my word, Percival, your curiosity exceeds mine. I have never taken upon me to inquire. Allow me to suggest that these questions require an explanation."

"That I can give frankly, or I should not have asked them. If you had said 'yes,' my path in life would have been decided. I have had an offer of missionary work, and should have accepted it at once."

Harcourt laid his hand on his shoulder.

"You are a good fellow, and I am very

sorry to hear you say this. I hoped you knew better. If you love my cousin, you do her great honour, for of the many who have admired her as she deserves, few have had half your worth and honesty of character. Between her and myself, I say at once, there has never been any engagement whatever, to give me a higher claim than you; nor have I any right to presume that I should be preferred to another. But, Percival, if I know either of you, such a woman is not the one to make you happy."

"Stop there. You may think it nothing to discuss your own relation and friend, but to me she is much more, and I will not hear a word that is not in her praise. If I have spoken openly to you, it is because my honour requires it. To her I have never spoken, and I do not know if I ever shall. I have nothing to offer her now that she would accept. I could not have remained here to see her your wife, but I can refrain from selfishly causing her annoyance, and I will. This is safe with you, I feel assured. Thank you."

"Wait a moment, Percival; let me understand you. If I had told you that I loved Stella Porchester, and hoped to win her, would that have been sufficient reason to you for sacrificing your own wishes?"

"It would have been enough to show me where my duty lay, and it would have been at my peril if I had neglected it. You have relieved my heart of a load—I wish I could relieve yours."

"I wish you could. Good-bye." Harcourt jumped over a gate leading into a wood, and was in a few moments out of sight.

Out of sight, but not of hearing, and Cecil listened to his receding footsteps, audible among the crackling boughs and dead leaves, some little time, before he turned slowly in another direction. Wild visions of hope flitted before his mind, as he glanced at the White House so conspicuous among the leafless trees. Would Stella Porchester indeed be satisfied to give up the life of variety and admiration to which she was accustomed, for the comparative monotony of a parsonage—and if she would, should he make peace with his uncle, and secure her a home at Durningham? This last involved a great deal, and was not to be thought of without a little preliminary argument. To be willing to put up with Mr. Holmby's dictation, poor old man, so utterly inadequate as he had become to meet the wants and claims of his parish, simply because he wished to marry, revolted him too much to be admitted. But the case looked different, when viewed in a different light. Mr. Brudenell had great influence with both Squire and Rector; what Holmby called new-fangled at Durningham, because past sloth and stupidity had parted with their privileges, was found no fault with at Stourbrooke. Julian Brudenell was the safe model always held up by those who coveted the epithet of "judicious." If he went back to Durningham supported by that authority and influence, and with all his good deeds at Stourbrooke as a proof of his fitness, then indeed—his heart beat more proudly again, for such a return would be a triumph, while the other would be a disgrace. And he thought of life passed in ever increasing usefulness and reputation—the highest offices in the Church open to his reach, and Stella, who had begun with him in comparative obscurity, finding herself repaid by increase of honour and distinction, which she should delight in owing to him. How golden looked the grey wintry landscape through this fairy medium—how impossible it seemed to come down at once from the sunny heights of fancy, to teach little girls in stuff frocks and holland pinafores! He could not give a lesson that day; he had too long neglected his old Durningham friends as it was; he would walk over now, and see the dear people who loved him so well, and who had stood by him against prejudice and misunderstanding—Mrs. Giles and Mrs. Allen, and good, well-meaning Miss Holmby, whom he had so patiently endured, in consideration of her kind intentions—he would walk over immediately, and gladden their hearts as well as his own. And away he went accordingly, and not a word could any one have said why he should not, if it had only occurred to him to let his little scholars know.

It must just be observed here that those who had expected to be amused with good stories of Cecil's revolutionary proceedings in Stourbrooke had hitherto been disappointed. The Vicar's behaviour towards his curate had been, from the first, such an appeal to his high breeding, that Percival would as soon have thought of attacking him in his own pulpit, as of going against his wishes in the parish. Where every suggestion he made met with courteous consideration, instead of repulse or ridicule, and his opinion was deferred to, whenever it could be proved that he was right, no inducement was left for beginning hasty schemes in a moment of excitement, and carrying them on afterwards because they were opposed. Something might be attributed to the growing passion which kept his imagination diverted to one particular subject, instead of expending itself in projects for the general weal; but there had been enough hard work during the epidemic to test his zeal and steadiness, and his conduct had justified Mr. Brudenell's confidence.

Lately, while the elders had so many sick to whom they wished to devote their time, the school had been left more than usual to their younger assistants; and Cecil and Marion had been regular visitors. And a sudden, but vivid conviction of the excessive dulness of the school routine, and the deplorable ignorance of the maidens of the rising generation, led to an announcement on Mr. Percival's part, one afternoon, of a course of lessons he proposed to give the girls, twice a week, at an hour specified, usually devoted to needlework. Anything being preferable in the opinion of some of those future helpmeets for man, to the sewing of linen and calico, or the mending of holes and tears, made (as if on purpose) by aggravating brothers at home—this proposal was received with grins of approval, and the next day he began his course on Natural Philosophy, which had now reached its fifth lesson. The first had been very popular; he took great pains to be simple in language, and lively in illustration, and his presence being in itself a joy to some sensitive members of the audience, who trembled all over with excitement if he only looked at them, they quite enjoyed the change from seams and patches, and had wonderful stories to tell to their small listeners at home. But as the novelty went off, and the words grew harder, and Mr. Percival talked faster, and grew impatient if he was not understood, things began to look more serious. An alarming discovery that they were expected to remember all they were told, so as to stand an examination next time, nearly reduced the school to despair; for though the questions were confined to the first class, all felt the consequences if the teacher grew vexed; and an angry look from Mr. Percival was something too heart-breaking to be encountered, if it were possible to avoid it. Yet how to answer such questions as he put, and expected to have answered, remained a problem, not easy of solution. Thankful were scholars and mistress, when, instead of the curate that afternoon, Miss Egerton came in, expecting to be just in time for the lesson.

Perhaps, of all his disciples, old or new, there was no one who by this time more thoroughly believed in Cecil than Marion Egerton. Like good Mrs. Black in the "Inheritance," she was still in the golden age of innocence, when belief in superiors is strong and lively; and both her uncle and his curate were in danger of falling short of the ideal excellence with which her imagination invested the English clergy. So good as they were, it naturally followed they must be perfect; and if Uncle Julian could do no wrong, it was becoming no less a rule, that Mr. Percival, with his zeal and devotedness, must pretty nearly always do right. Though quick at discerning false from true, she was sanguine in belief that what was true when spoken, would prove itself so in deeds; and wondered at the incredulity of her aunt when she came home with her heart glowing with hopefulness touching the amendment of some sadly lax old neighbour, who had given vent to one of her periodical fits of remorse to the dear young creature who spoke so kind, and who really did mean to begin—well, not to-morrow, my dear, because it was market-day, you see, and she'd be all day long on her feet, and tired to death—but come Sunday next, and she really would make herself tidy, and go to church, that would she; it would do her a power of good, she was sure. It did Marion so much good to come home and promise that Goody Grice was turning over a new leaf, that it was a sad shock to be told it was the tenth she had turned at the very least, and that each had proved rather worse than its predecessors. But even proofs of the accuracy of the statement had not yet taught her the too painful lesson—a lesson some of her own past experiences might have helped her to learn—that to see and know what is right is not always to do it.

Her ready belief and docile obedience made her invaluable as a follower to so exacting a teacher as Cecil. To her, in Roland's absence, he relieved himself by pouring out his schemes, his opinions, his altering views, and his high aspirations, as fast as they appeared or altered in his own mind; and if she could not always implicitly agree, or even understand, she almost always admired, and listened with respect, eager to learn, and longing to imitate. She worked untiringly at everything he gave her to do, unaware how often Mrs. Brudenell, sooner than have her darling overtasked, refrained from employing her herself, when she would have been glad of her help. And more than once had she fought his battles, when some new notion of his, somewhat vehemently obtruded, was discussed at the Vicarage tea-table; her uncle pretending sometimes much more hostility than he meant, for the amusement of seeing her ruffle up in his defence.

As to the present matter in hand, she had heard from Cecil so much about the fatal waste of intellect among the poorer class of women—he had spoken so powerfully on the change that would be brought about by giving those hard-worked housewives, servants, and mothers, something true and ennobling to think of, in the ordinary phenomena of everyday life—he had described so graphically the ruinous results of ignorance in neglect of the simplest sanitary rules, and wilful carelessness in cooking their food—that she had only been able to acquiesce, and commend, and think how fortunate the parish was to have one so ready, and so capable of giving the necessary teaching. So she went to the Natural Philosophy lesson when she could; but having other duties, missed the last, and had been too busy with her own class in the morning to inquire about it. She was not prepared, therefore, for the state of collapse in which she found the school this day. Miss Poole, the mistress, a methodical, efficient person in her own line, but quite lost in any other, had been putting the elder girls through a preliminary examination, which had brought out some startling results; and as it appeared that the pupils who did remember anything, had each understood something different, and the mistress differed from them all, as a whole it could hardly be called satisfactory. So all turned eagerly to Marion—the girls with that unlimited belief in young ladies' knowledge, which school children generally have—the mistress, in a somewhat injured tone, to relieve herself of a grievance.

"You see, Miss Egerton, if Mr. Percival had only been good enough to bring me the book he promised, relating to the lesson, I could have taken care the children remembered it; but he teaches them out of his own head, with only the chalk and the board, and tells them a great deal at once, and expects them to answer questions off like print when he comes again. Now really, ma'am, this is rather hard upon us all, and if I could do it without the book I would; but it is what I do not pretend to teach myself, and I must speak to Mrs. Brudenell if it goes on, I must indeed."

Marion was sorry—hoped it was only for once—recommended trying once more, and offered help. What had the lesson been about? The question was put to the girls; they looked at each other, and some tittered, but no one answered at first. At last one said, "Please, 'm, the kettle."

"It wasn't, Sarah Jane, it was the teapot."

"It was both, please, 'm, and the fire too, and how you could put a fire out, by putting a pocket-handkercher into it."

"No, *on* it, Lucy—how can you!——"

"But it don't, please, 'm, for I tried with our Bill's, and it frizzled it all up in a minute, and he *was* just cross."

"And please, 'm, he said the best tea was made by having the teapot black and smoky—he did, Sarah Jane!—and he said we was to try for ourselves, and me and Betsey did, please, 'm, with the new chaney teapot Mrs. Brudenell gave to granny."

"And was it better than usual?" asked Marion, whom this volley of facts began to alarm.

"I don't know, please, 'm, 'cause the teapot cracked in two."

"Now, children, do not talk so fast, all at once," interposed the mistress; "you deafen Miss Egerton. But if you please, ma'am, there is one thing they declare Mr. Percival said, which I cannot believe—I was busy with the little ones at the time—that they ought to wear white frocks and bonnets in hot weather. White frocks in a school, ma'am—I cannot conceive how a gentleman could imagine it possible—they would not be tidy an hour, and as to the washing, their mothers never could manage it. Why, dear me, their print frocks get inked and dirtied fast enough; what they would be if they wore white muslins, I cannot pretend to say."

"White muslin! I should think not, indeed. There must have been some mistake."

"I think so too, Miss Egerton; you'll excuse my saying there has been more than one mistake, and I really must speak to Mrs. Brudenell, unless you would be good enough to do so, for here is a whole afternoon gone, and the Vicar's shirts not finished, and the girls all unsettled, and their mothers finding fault with me. I cannot see the good it does them, and I cannot pretend to teach such things, only leading them into mischief. There is that child, ma'am—she may well hide herself behind Carry Simpson—as nearly as possible scalded herself and her brother to death, trying to put a cork in the spout of the tea-kettle, to see if it would blow the roof off. You would hardly believe it, ma'am, of such children as that, that they should be so keen upon mischief—but her aunt told it me herself. It is a mercy they are both alive."

Marion thought so too, but mildly suggested that some explanation of all these curious illustrations must have been given in the lecture, and was at once directed to the board, whereon glared in the eyes of the school the terrible words, "RADIATION—CONVECTION—CONDUCTION—COMBUSTION," with sundry diagrams in white chalk, carefully preserved from the last lesson, but only to be regarded with wondering dismay. If Miss Egerton understood them, there was a hope left, and all eyes stared at her, as she stood looking at the board.

And at that most ill-chosen moment, who should come into the school but Mrs. Brudenell, and old Mr. Holmby, the Rector of Durningham. Miss Poole grew scarlet with annoyance, uttered signals that were at first hardly heeded, and could only by strenuous gestures restore anything like order to the arrangement of the pupils; while Marion, conscious how much handle was given to criticism, buckled on her armour in haste to defend her colours. They were expecting Mr. Percival every minute, to give them a lesson, she explained, before any comment could be made, and were talking it over before he came, otherwise they would all have been quietly seated at their work. Should Miss Poole show Mr. Holmby some of their needlework? Really, some of the girls had improved very much in their stitching, and Miss Poole took a great deal of pains. And fervently did she hope the conversation would take so decided a turn in the direction of seam, and gusset, and band, as would postpone all mention of Natural Philosophy for the present. Mrs. Brudenell, however, was in no hurry to make an exhibition of performances; she had brought the old Rector in to see the size of the room, as his own was out of repair, and the Squire had volunteered to build a new one on the pattern of Stourbrooke. The discussion of height and length and breadth gave mistress and scholars breathing-time; Miss Poole's cheeks and nose were regaining their ordinary colour, and Marion hoped all would pass without notice, or that Percival would come in to manage his own affairs. However, she was destined to be disappointed, for in the midst of a history of the rain coming through the roof, and the sight of money that had been spent on the building from first to last, it being a ramshackle concern originally—Mr. Holmby turned to observe, in his loud, tremulous voice, "I met Percival as I came, but he did not see me; he was tearing across the fields just as I drove down the road. He is gone to see my sister, I hope; she is very fond of him, though they'll argue on Brady and Tate by the hour together."

"Gone to Durningham, is he?" said Mrs.

Brudenell, with a demure glance at her niece. "Don't you think, my dear, they might as well get to their sewing at once?"

"Certainly," said Marion, biting her lip, as she detected a sarcastic smile on that of Miss Poole. "Indeed," she added rather petulantly, "I think they had always better go on working till the lesson begins. It is impossible for Mr. Percival to be punctual to a minute."

"So it appears," said Mrs. Brudenell, drily. "When is the Vicar to have his shirts, Miss Poole?"

"Indeed, ma'am, that is more than I can take upon me to say, if we are interrupted as we have been lately," was Miss Poole's quick retort on Miss Egerton's last observation; "the children's time is so much taken up with other things."

"What is all that about?" here demanded the old Rector, pointing with his cane at the unlucky board. "Spelling lesson, hey? Let's hear how you can do it. Stand up, you Laura Matilda, or whatever your name is—if I pick out a fine one, I am pretty sure to be right—stand up, and spell it to me. Speak out, for I am a little deaf."

Sarah Jane rose reluctantly; her eyes rolling on Miss Egerton in despair. "You can spell that word, I am sure," said Marion, in the blandest tone of encouragement, and wishing Miss Holmby had been anywhere before she lured the curate away on that particular afternoon.

"Of course she can," added Mrs. Brudenell; "start off, Sarah, and do us credit."

So Sarah Jane started off, and spelt, in all its due syllables, the dreaded Radiation.

"Well done," said the old gentleman; "now for the meaning."

"Tell Mr. Holmby what it means," said Mrs. Brudenell.

The child glared at Marion, and was evidently on the verge of a howl. Marion threw herself into the breach.

"They have not learned the meaning quite yet, sir," she said, but not quite loudly enough for Mr. Holmby to hear, who replied, "Not know it yet? Pass on to another. Here, you Clementina Jacquelina, take her down, and give us the meaning."

But Betsey looked even more hopeless than her predecessor. "It is not a spelling lesson at all, sir," shouted Marion, now scarlet in her turn.

"Not a spelling lesson, my dear? Oh! What is it, then? A copy? Let us see, let us see—I am a great judge of pothooks and hangers."

"No, sir—not a copy. They were going to have a lesson on Natural Philosophy."

"On *what?*"

"On Natural Philosophy, sir. Mr. Percival teaches them, but I suppose he could not come to-day."

The old gentleman stared at her through his spectacles, nearly as hard as the children had done. "Teaches them Natural Philosophy, does he? Oh!" He took his spectacles off, and rubbed them significantly. "I should like to hear what they have been learning, for I cannot say that any philosophy comes very natural to me, and it is the first time I heard it did to him. Suppose they tell us a little about it. Begin, you Sophonisba."

He had put his spectacles on again, and his old eyes twinkled behind them, as he observed the alarm of the school, and the offended attitude of the mistress. Marion, desperate at the idea of the teapot and kettle being paraded before so hostile a critic, whispered imploringly to her aunt; and Mrs. Brudencll at once interposed, protesting that she knew better than to allow her children to be examined by such a judge, unprepared; if he came over after Christmas, they might then be ready to show off,—meanwhile, they should be happy to sing to him instead. And joyful for the reprieve, the girls fell into their places immediately, and sang his favourite tunes, which Cecil had not yet attempted to banish, till they had forgotten their troubles, and he his little bit of malice.

Profiting by the opportunity, Miss Egerton made her escape, and in the darkening twilight of the brief winter afternoon, walked back to her home. She had promised Percival that a certain number of chants should be copied out from a collection he had borrowed of a friend; and this interval before tea was just the time she had relied on, for accomplishing the task. As she entered the Vicarage gate, a dog jumped upon her; it was Roland's favourite, Nelson, and Harcourt was close behind.

"Is your uncle at home, Miss Egerton? Down, Nelson, sir! May I come in and wait for him? I have had rather a long walk."

She could not but make him welcome, and would have brought Nelson in too, but he knew better, and lay down at the gate, as Roland had taught him. Marion lingered to caress his sleek head, and bring him water, and sweet biscuits, filched from Jane's private stores; and Harcourt watched her so doing, and half smiled at himself for feeling for once like Colonel Gardiner. They went into the parlour, and she threw a log on the fire, and drew an arm-chair forward, and made him sit down and rest; he would excuse her going on with what she had promised to do—she could talk and listen just the same. And she opened her music-book, and began rapidly transcribing the notes, thinking the kindest thing to a man so tired as he was, would be to show him there was no occasion for him to talk.

The firelight played on her shining hair and blooming cheek; and he was content, at first, to recline in silence, and watch her as she wrote, following every movement of the small busy fingers, every turn of the bright head, that had become to him so fatally dear. Could he ever have imagined they would be so—or that a day would come when he should feel, in utter bitterness of soul, it had been better for him to have died as Saville died, than to have accepted his dying charge? There she sat, unconscious of what was coming; too accustomed to his presence to be disturbed by the recollection of what had passed between them, remembered only as an instance of his chivalrous generosity. She had never thought he loved her, but that he believed her destitute, and offered her a home—whether instigated thereto by his own compassion solely she had never dared to investigate—and her uncle and aunt had encouraged the opinion, without divulging Harcourt's secret. That his affection had been really won, never occurred to either of the three.

It grew dark before Marion had finished her first page, and she was about to ring for a light, but he interposed. "Do me a favour, and wait a few minutes. This firelight is so soothing, and I am sure you want a little rest too. You looked as if you did when I came up to you."

"I had been a little vexed, but that is over now; I am not tired. You must leave off thinking of me as a convalescent, for I never was in better health."

"I am sorry for it; I wish I could give you a relapse. I like you best as an invalid."

"Thank you, but I prefer being well to looking interesting. I gave you all quite trouble enough as it was."

"You will never know half the trouble you gave."

She shook her head. "That I can quite believe; but some day I may have my turn, and be able to take trouble for you. I find it no grievance to owe more than I can repay."

"Marion," he said, in a low, pleading voice, "if I thought, by exposing myself to suffering and danger, I should make you feel towards me what I have felt for you, you might be called upon to do your part to-morrow."

There was something in his tone as he called her by her name that touched her too much to give offence or alarm; she felt sorry, very sorry for him, for she feared he was in depressed spirits, but she could not reply to such a speech, and regretted having allowed the conversation to take a personal turn. He, on the other hand, felt that the die was cast, and rising from his chair, and leaning against the mantelpiece, with his head bent down near to hers, he poured out his love—not with that calm, tender gentleness with which he had wooed her before, but with the almost despairing earnestness of a man who pleads for his life. A little more, and he was kneeling by her side, almost crouching at her feet. "Marion, Marion, say you do not quite refuse me—give me only the hope that I may win you at last!"

She had tried to make him listen several times, but in vain; now he had seized her hand, and she felt how burning hot was that which grasped it, and how fierce was the strength of the grasp in which she was so utterly powerless. But she saw that at all hazards he must be convinced, and mastered her own agitation and fear sufficiently to speak with decision.

"Mr. Clarendon, listen to me—I entreat you to listen to me, and quietly, or I shall consider this an insult."

"There is no insult in a man's telling a woman he loves her, except when his words are untrue—and you know mine are not."

"I am sure they are not; I honour and esteem you too well to doubt it."

"Honour and esteem me—for what, Marion? Do you know what I am doing now? Do you know that I am wronging as tender a confidence as was ever reposed in man, and doing all the injury in my power to one I have loved for years, and can never replace from this hour? If you did, you would know, too, that though you might love me for the sake of my love, you could neither honour nor esteem me again. I know the worst that can be said, that can be thought, of my conduct; but the truth remains the same—I cannot give you up to another. I will make you love me, Marion, in spite of yourself; I will make you so happy, I will enable you to do so much good, I will fill your life with so many pleasures, innocent, rational, elevating pleasures, that you shall bless me, night and morning, for winning you, and only pray for me, that I may deserve you more!"

"It cannot, cannot be," she said, as steadily as she could. "I know you are a generous friend; I have thought of you as such, and if you did but ask what was in my power—but I cannot deceive you, or pretend to love you, when——"

She could not finish the sentence, but he started to his feet as if the words had been spoken. "When you love another better—is that what you meant to say?"

"You have no right to ask me!" she replied, with spirit, while the tears sprang to her eyes. Her courage had begun to fail, and she was longing for her aunt to come in, when they were both startled by a familiar sound at the gate. It was Nelson's joyful bark, and Roland's voice quieting him.

"Why, old fellow, what are you doing here at this hour? Good taste, I must say. Here, Nancy! are the ladies at home?"

Nancy's answer was inaudible; Harcourt, who had turned white as he listened, snatched up his hat, and with one look at Marion—a look she remembered long afterwards—was just in time to stop Roland from coming in. "They are engaged—they cannot see you now—come home," he repeated, rapidly and imperatively, linking his arm in his brother's, and almost forcing him again into the road. His manner was so strange, Roland almost forgot the disappointment. "What is the matter? Did you get my letter?"

"Yes, yes; I got it, of course. What has brought you down to-day?"

"Oh, I was introduced by Sir Perkin's nephew, and my chief is a good-natured fellow, who knows him well, and I fancy they had both had a hint that I had not passed badly, and ought to have rest; and so, when I screwed up my courage to ask if it mattered whether I began work a week later or not, he laughed, and said he thought they might make shift to manage without me for a few days; so I rushed home to pack, left old Gervase to make my excuses in half a dozen places, and took the next train."

"What made you go to the Vicarage instead of coming straight home?"

"I did not intend to call, but, you see, as I was walking from the station, I could not resist passing the windows, just on the chance. What had taken *you* there, by the way?"

"I had a question to ask; we will talk it all

over by-and-by. Here come our good friends," as Mr. and Mrs. Brudenell, having parted with Mr. Holmby, emerged from a cottage they had been visiting together.

Roland stepped forward to shake hands. "Give me joy, Mrs. Brudenell, of my first holiday."

"I am more likely to give you joy on getting something to do. Holiday! Why, you have had nothing else all your life, ever since I have known you."

"Then now my working time has begun; I have every prospect of rising, I assure you. I say, may I call to-morrow morning, to speak on an important subject? May I come to breakfast?"

"If you will promise not to show your nose in the kitchen, for eggs are scarce, and Jane will be busy."

"I have no intention of intruding on Jane. Expect me after Church. I hope Miss Egerton is quite well?"

"I hope so too, but I doubt it. Upon my word, that boy Cecil is enough to drive any one crazy, and to see Marion's face this afternoon was as good as a play. We will tell you all about it to-morrow. Good-bye."

The Vicar and his wife walked on, and the

brothers pursued their way in silence; Roland pondering what the last remark could mean.

"Jealous, are you, Roland?" asked Harcourt.

"Not at all; Cecil knows my sentiments, and would have been the first to give me warning. Noll, you have not yet said a word about my letter—you must know how anxious I am."

"I have a great deal to say to you, and would rather say it at home," was all the reply; and nothing more was said on either side.

On going up to his room, Roland was surprised to meet Trail, in plain clothes, at Harcourt's door. "Why, what office are you supposed to fill now?" he asked, in that supercilious tone with which he never could help addressing this obnoxious *protégé;* "I left you a groom—what is your new character?"

"Mr. Clarendon has engaged me as his valet, sir, to his entire satisfaction, as well as mine."

"He always declared he never would keep a valet, and this is a choice beginning, but he must please himself. Have you given up the fine arts, then?"

"By no means, sir; my master is good

enough to give me every opportunity of improving my taste."

"He had better improve his own," said Roland, turning on his heel with his hands thrust into his pockets, tingling with the keen desire he felt to fling the man down stairs. How his brother could take such a fancy to the fellow, he could not conceive, and it was with some difficulty he refrained from broaching the subjects till the servants had left them alone to their wine. Then he abruptly expressed his surprise, observing that to put such a fellow as that in a place of trust and temptation really seemed ridiculous.

"What could I do?" asked Harcourt, carelessly; "he could not ride decently—I took him out with me once, and the whole field laughed at his seat; he has no muscles for work, and he is quiet and handy about me, amuses me with his airs, and sometimes with his adventures. I consider him a natural curiosity; his memory is something wonderful, and his faculty of telling lies might serve as a model for an Oriental diplomatist."

"He should not tell one twice in my hearing, if he were my servant."

"Oh! you are too scrupulous—you expect truth and honour everywhere; now you are a

Government official, you will soon be cured of that weakness."

"With my brother I am safe, at any rate. Harcourt, you said you would speak when we were alone. I can bear it no longer—tell me at once what you have to say."

He had noticed already that Harcourt had scarcely tasted any of the dishes handed to him, though he partook freely of the wine; and now, watching his face more narrowly, he could see it was working with agitation. He drew his chair nearer, and stretched his hand across the table.

"We have always been frank with each other, Noll, and I can truly say there is not a thought or wish of mine I would keep secret from you."

"I wish you had never said a word to me about it; if you could only have kept it to yourself like a man, I should feel more like one now. Roland, do you remember my begging you to leave us, that first night at Baden?"

"Yes; you had some reason then, I admit. Now——"

"I have more. It is impossible—you ask what I cannot give. I would do anything on earth that was reasonable—I would share this estate with you, if that would be enough; or if you preferred, buy you a farm, or make you a handsome settlement, instead of an allowance——"

"If you talk like that, I shall think you mean to insult me. What is it you cannot do?"

"I cannot give you up Marion Egerton."

CHAPTER III.

DIVIDED.

PERCIVAL was sitting up later than usual, transcribing from a very blotted and confused pile of MSS. a sermon for the following Sunday—an operation which cost him an amount of labour by no means generally appreciated. His fastidious and variable taste led him to revise and retouch every sentence several times over, and, when all was done, to the simple majority of the congregation it was pains thrown away. Mrs. Brudenell used to tell him so, by way, as she thought, of lessening his conceit; but the Vicar, if at hand, would always defend the practice, as showing a resolution to give the best work to the Master's cause. His own sermons were less laboured with the pen, because they were the result of a life's labour in the study. For the study our energetic curate never seemed to have time, and his compositions had to be drawn from the resources already stored up; and any one who does this long without renewing his stores, knows what hard work it becomes at last. With weary fingers and burning eyes, he was forcing himself to complete his task before going to bed, when a handful of gravel thrown up against his window-pane, startled him from his occupation. He threw up the sash, and looked out. A tall figure was just visible in the faint starlight.

"Any one ill?" asked Cecil. He had grown accustomed of late to be summoned at all hours, and had given special orders always to send to him at night, instead of to the Vicar.

"No—it is I—Roland. Can you let me in?"

There was no joyous ring in that hoarse voice, and a nameless dread crept over the listener. Something was the matter—not sorrow, or it would have spoken out at once; had that frank, happy nature been suddenly led astray, and was he come to pour his remorse out in confession to his friend? The thought made him shiver, as he hurried down, candle in hand, to admit the unexpected visitor.

"Do not disturb my landlord," he whispered,

without expressing any surprise; "he works hard all day, poor man. Come up with me—I am glad I happened to be still out of bed."

Roland followed him silently to his room; the curate lighted an additional candle, put coals on his dying fire, and emptied an arm-chair of a pile of books with which it had been gradually filled. Mrs. Brudenell might insist on his having such a chair, but she could not make him sit in it, so long as it was heaped with other things.

"Sit down, Clarendon, and tell me what you will have. You are just off a journey, of course, and started without any dinner. I have an apparatus here, constructed after a plan of my own, that can brew you a cup of coffee, or cook up a basin of stiff soup, in five minutes."

"Thank you—I have dined. I dined at Morlands."

"Why, when did you arrive?"

"This afternoon."

"I met your brother to-day, and he did not mention that you were expected."

"I was not expected, and, what is more, Percival, it will be a long time before I shall be expected at Morlands again. You may as well know the whole at once—my brother and I have quarrelled."

"Heaven forbid!" said Percival, more shocked by his tone than by the intelligence, which he considered only the exaggeration of a passing resentment.

"Heaven has forbidden it, and pretty strongly too," returned the other, "but it does not alter the fact."

"You are not quite yourself to-night, my dear fellow, or you would not speak in such a manner," said the curate. "I can see you have been very much vexed and hurt by something, and if I can help you, I will. My means are not large, but if there is anything within their compass that can lift you out of a difficulty, or pull you through a scrape, you know it is yours, as if you were my brother."

"Brother?" repeated Roland, too excited for gratitude, or even acknowledgment, "I have no brother—a brother would not have treated me as I have been treated, and only learned to-night. Did I ever complain to any one of my father's will? Did I ever grumble because one had all, and the other nothing? I have had it thrust upon my notice perpetually by other people, and I never gave it a thought. It is no disgrace to take an allowance from a father, and I felt it none to receive it from Harcourt. It was a pleasure to know how he enjoyed giving me all I wished for. I should as soon have dreamed of a child on its mother's lap coming to terms and settlements with her, as of being disturbed about his doing me justice. And what has he done, by his own showing? From the first, I told him of my attachment to Miss Egerton—he knew it in Switzerland, he knew it better still at Baden—he did not like the idea, on account of Mr. Saville, and he did all he could to keep us apart. I bore that, because I was sure the more he saw of her, the more convinced he must be that I was right; I little knew what the end would be. Saville died—left her in his charge—and he sends me off to England directly, to get me out of the way. And why? Because he was all the while endeavouring to win her for himself."

"You are dreaming," cried Cecil, his heart bounding with hope and fear.

"I wish I were! I was dreaming until to-night; now I am awake to my bitter sorrow. I came down, as he knew, for I wrote to tell him I should, to learn my fate; I have now a fair prospect, and can honestly go to Brudenell and ask his consent; and I find——"

His voice was almost choked, and it was some minutes before he could resume more calmly. "In a word, we are rivals, and not only so, but he has acted in an underhand manner, dishonouring us both. Before Marion

Egerton left Morlands, he had asked her to be his wife, and after receiving my letter to-day, he asked her again."

"That was what he meant when he appealed to me," murmured Cecil, with a pang of remorse, as he recollected his answer. "If I had but known!"

"Who could know? Whom would any one trust if not Harcourt? I would have staked my life on his honour and truth. Even now, he is so far true, that he told me all this himself, and he would buy off my claims at my own price—faugh! Half the property, Percival, if I will only postpone asking Marion; I can then choose again—the world will be open before me, and perhaps I shall be all the happier. Likely, is it not, that a man would take money in exchange for the joy and hope of his life? He would not do it himself, neither will I."

"He loves Miss Egerton, then, in real earnest?"

"Who could help loving her? I was an idiot, not to see it before, but I really thought——"

"Hush—we need bring in no other subject till we have done with this. You said all you could, no doubt; I am afraid, rather too hastily."

"No, we were cool for some time, for I was

slow of belief, and thought he did not realise what it was to me. I did not lose my temper till the end; but when it came to this, that he would never consent to, or assist me in such an union, I told him that until he did, I would accept no gift, or favour, or obligation from his hands — I would not eat his bread, or sleep under his roof, neither would I touch a farthing more of his money. He has disgraced himself and me, and till he owns it, we are as strangers, let it cost me what it will."

It was no use attempting to argue with such a resolution as this, in such a frame; and Percival only soothed him by sympathy, and endeavoured to persuade him to occupy his bed, hoping that a short sleep might make him more amenable to advice. Sleep was, however, impossible in Roland's excited state, and he sat with his friend till morning, sometimes in weary silence—sometimes beginning afresh, and going over the whole ground again—Percival listening with the patience of true affection, and revolving in his mind at intervals how he could best heal the breach before it had gone further. What the effect on his own hopes might be, he would not allow himself to consider.

Morning came at last, and unrested as the

curate was, it behoved him to do his work; and having accommodated his guest with the means of a hasty toilet, he prevailed on him to accompany him to the service, which Roland, miserable as he was, would have missed. The more miserable, the more fit, argued his adviser,—the rather that he was afraid to leave him alone; and accordingly, the tall figure and haggard face were full in view when Marion came in with her aunt. A deadly fear stole over her heart. It was well she had the service as a support, for she felt some terrible crisis was at hand, and needed all it could give her. Whether Roland prayed or not, it were difficult to say; to him the whole world was changed, and with it, his own nature. Hard, angry, bitter thoughts rushed thickly, one upon another, when he saw how pale Marion looked, as if she, too, had passed an agitated night; and thought of his glad hopes yesterday. "Forgive us our trespasses," in the Vicar's clear, sweet voice, thrilled on his ear, but not in his heart; he shut its doors against the gentle visitant; he was angry, even unto death, and he would not forgive, or yield, no, not an inch. He, too, could stand firm, where the right was on his side, and all the world should know it.

The service ended, he joined the ladies, and

they all tried to speak in the painfully cheerful tone which people assume on such occasions. Oh yes, he was coming to breakfast, and it would be a treat to taste milk once more, without the flavour of the metropolitan pump —not to mention other condiments, on which he was beginning a popular story, but broke it off abruptly, when he observed how earnestly Cecil was speaking to the Vicar, as they issued from the vestry door. He was sure Mr. Brudenell knew all, by the tender pressure he gave his hand; and felt a wild, boyish longing to throw himself in his arms, and give vent to the passion of grief and rage now choking in his breast. But such things are rarely done among Englishmen, and he walked on, and talked very fast, and was so unlike himself, in his straining after intense liveliness of spirits all breakfast-time, that it was a relief to the whole party when they rose from table. The Vicar, as they did so, put his hand on his niece's shoulder. "My love, will you do me the kindness to go into my study, and copy out three letters you will find lying together on the table?"

It was always a great honour for Marion to be asked to assist her uncle, and she did not hesitate; though it just crossed her mind that he might have waited till Roland was gone.

The dining-room door closed behind her, as she hurried to the study and began her task, finding it very difficult to refrain from impatience, and still more from harassing conjectures. She detected herself reading the same words over five or six times, without taking in their meaning, while revolving the questions that had kept her awake half the night, and could not be answered till she knew more. She was unhappy about Harcourt, and yet there was joy in knowing Roland was so near; and it never occurred to her that she could be a real cause of division between them. The dread that made her heart throb, though unacknowledged even to herself, was that the younger might feel it his duty to withdraw in favour of the elder; he had never spoken openly of love, however expressive had been his looks and actions, and he might feel that honour and gratitude required the sacrifice, which, as far as he knew, might be on his side only. As far as he knew—and yet, did he not know the truth? Had not their intercourse from the first been so sweet to both, that the future had become blended with images of union, without which it would be a desolate blank? Had not his name been on her lips that very morning, the foremost among the few for whom she prayed as we only pray for our soul's hidden treasures—and could anything compensate to her now, for the loss of the hope that had given it a right to be there?

So she mused, and wrote perseveringly the while, with no more idea of what she was writing, than the good people to whom the letters were destined would have of the emotions of the transcriber. They took longer than she expected, and she had just written the last "(Signed) Julian Brudenell," when the study door opening, admitted, as she thought, Julian Brudenell himself.

"I have just done," she said, without turning her head; "I hope I have not made many mistakes."

There was no answer, but a step across the room that was not her uncle's; and Roland came and sat down by her side. "Never mind how many mistakes you may have made in your letters," he said, with the smile that she had learned to think so irresistible, "only let there be none between us now."

It was as well that Marion's task was finished, as it would be difficult to conjecture, after thi[s] opening, what liberties she might not hav[e] taken with the original text. As she laid dow[n] her pen, Roland took possession of her hand.

"Your uncle and aunt have allowed me [t]o [see] you now," he went on, "and th only stipulate that you should know everything. I can have but one wish on that point, and if I had had my own way, you would have been told everything before. But after what I heard you say about idle men, and all that was dinned into my ears on that score in this house, I made up my mind not to speak till I had given proof of my good intentions. The hope of this moment made up to me for all the dull hours I have been sapping in London, giving up hunting and everything—and I have really passed very well, they say, and have every prospect of getting on, and I do mean to do my duty, and work as hard as the best."

"I am sure you will," said Marion, as he paused for a moment.

"Then may I speak out now?" and as he talked of speaking out, his voice dropped lower, almost in her ear. "Is it necessary to tell you what you must have found out for yourself, that I have cared for nothing in comparison with you since the first day I saw you in Paris? It was entirely for the chance of meeting you again I followed you to Interlachen, and remained with you all afterwards; and every hour in your company made me love you more. I was very nearly telling you so that evening in the Allée; I think you must have guessed it, even then. And I have hoped we understood each other, even though we did not speak. You are truth itself; you could not deceive if you would—tell me if I may hope?"

She had no wish to deceive him; her eyes were eloquent in their reply; and the possibility of there being any mistake seemed too minute to be worth mentioning. She had understood, or hoped she did, but she was glad to be assured by his own lips of what was so sweet to know, and which he found so sweet to tell; and though he took a long time to tell it, she did not find the topic wearisome, or the speaker too diffuse in style. Perhaps he lingered the longer on this sunny side of the path, from the consciousness of the dark shadow lowering near, into which she must pass by his side; yet, linger and delay as he might, the whole had not yet been told, and he was pledged to tell it without reserve. So he named Harcourt, and felt the hand he held press his own nervously.

"You know what has passed?" she said, in a low voice.

"Yes, I know that he has endeavoured to supplant me—me, who confided in him from the beginning—and that he has failed. I don't blame him for loving you—who could help it? but he has acted shabbily by me, and therefore I would not sleep under his roof last night."

"You have not quarrelled?—he loves you so dearly, and has been so good to me!"

"We have had such a quarrel as men can only have once; and unless he alters, it will be for life."

"No, Roland, no—not between brothers."

"Is it less of an injury to be wronged by your brother than by any other man?"

"Not less of an injury, but easier to forgive. Think a moment—we have each other—he will be alone, caring for both, and having neither. Do not let me think I have been the means of dividing you, as a return for all the kindness I have received."

"You do not think any blame can attach to you. Tears in those dear eyes, darling? I can bear anything better than that. What do you wish me to do? Have you any idea of what he has been offering, to induce me, at any rate, to put off telling you I loved you? He would have given me whatever I chose to ask, only to buy himself a respite, and a chance; but consent to our marriage he will not. And it came to this at last, that until he does, and acts and speaks as a brother should, I will not accept a farthing from his purse, or taste a crust from his table. So long as he behaved to me like himself, I thought no more of being beholden to him than to my father; but this alters the case, and I would sooner starve than let him give me a shilling."

Long and seriously did they talk this over; for let Marion soften matters as she might, she could not change the position of affairs, or avoid seeing that an engagement to Roland, supported by the affection of his wealthy brother, was a very different prospect from that of one formed under existing circumstances, his salary being as modest as his hopes of promotion and competence were bold. He laid it all plainly before her, as he had promised he would, and as he might safely do, for marvels of prudence are not common at two or three and twenty. She thought more of the breach between the brothers than of the loss involved therein, and would not see that a reconciliation must, in the very face of it, be at present impossible. Harcourt was generous and noble; he had been peculiarly generous to her; if he had spoken bitterly under the influence of disappointment, he would master himself in time, so long as he was not goaded by reproach, or repulsed by enmity. Better they should wait for years, if necessary, than that Roland should lose his brother and his home on her account. And when he repeated that all were well lost if she were gained, she felt it was very sweet to have won such love, but that he might one day think he had purchased hers too dearly.

"Let us consult my uncle and aunt," was the suggestion that was the easiest to make him agree to, and most comforting to herself. She knew they would do anything for her happiness, and that their advice was sure to be on the side of right; and so the case was carried again to the anxious elders, who had been in earnest consultation in the interval, unable to attend to, or think of anything else. They had long loved Roland, and they dearly loved Marion, and if they could have settled an annuity upon them at once, and let them be happy then and there, they would have done it; but what Mr. Brudenell had saved, his wife would need at his death, and it would only be a small assistance he could promise his niece. The chance of her regaining any part of her lost fortune was very remote indeed, so that her two thousand pounds were all the dowry she had to bring. Roland inherited from his mother a sum in the funds, of rather more than equal amount; so that, taking the most favourable view of their joint circumstances, as to interest and salary, they could not make up much more than three hundred a year between them—a poor prospect for London expenses. An immediate or speedy marriage was out of the question, unless some provision were made by Harcourt. This the Vicar maintained he ought, and probably would admit he ought to make; and Roland steadily protested he would not accept it if it were offered. Would it then be wise or right to enter on so indefinite an engagement? That question, it was submitted, came too late; they had allowed Marion to decide, and she had decided, and if they must wait, at any rate it would be easier to do so with an engagement than without it. It need not be so long as they thought—Roland had made friends, in a position to give him a lift, and as soon as he was back in town, he should stir them all up. Very soon, they would see, he should be pushed into a good berth. He had no fears about the future, now that he might call Marion his own.

He might have no fears, and in her presence he might have no real trouble, but, considering that he had always contrived, as his friends well knew, to get through more than the utmost they could reckon upon as a possible income, on his own little private expenses, the whole thing did not tend to raise the spirits of the Vicar or his wife. Mr. Brudenell finally closed the discussion by announcing that he must think it all over, and see what could be done, after he had spoken to Harcourt; and so saying, he took his hat and walked out, leaving the lovers to his wife.

He felt keenly on the subject, for the two young men had each his own particular place in his heart, and Marion, though a late comer, had special claims of her own. But for George Saville's conduct, she would now have been independent enough to marry whom she pleased, and it would be an additional wrong, if the son of Saville's friend should withhold that justice which would in some measure make compensation. So, before he went to Morlands, he took a solitary walk down a retired lane, in which he had often found inspiration, when the Muse, if such there be, who presides over sermon writing, failed him utterly at home. It was muddy and dull enough to break an author's heart who went there to be inspired, but that did not trouble the good man, who was used to mud, and uninfluenced by dulness. He wanted to think the whole matter over quietly, and there was no place so secure from interruption.

But where is that secure spot in the world in which security from interruption can be guaranteed? There was one cottage in this lane, inhabited by a labourer's family; and as Mr. Brudenell came within sight, a figure stepped out, and advanced to meet him. Not having on his spectacles, he did not at first recognise the said figure, as he came jauntily along, swinging a little cane in one hand—the other stuck on his hip; but as it approached, he saw it was Mr. Trail. The artist was passing with a graceful salute, à la Claude Melnotte, but Mr. Brudenell stopped him short.

"Are you going straight back to Morlands?"

"As straight, sir, as the meandering of the road will permit me."

"And as your old habit will permit you," said the Vicar, in a tone that, for him, was almost stern. "Foolish fellow, have you not bought your experience yet?"

"Bought heaps of it, sir, but it doesn't wear well, and that's the truth. Couldn't keep up to the mark, sir, at any price, without a slight stimulus. It in no ways interferes with my duty, and my master has never found fault with my personal conduct."

"No; if he did so once, it would be for the last time. Take care, Trail—you are dealing with a generous man, who will bear with you longer than many would, because you are under his protection; but if he once passes judgment upon you, your chance is gone. He will not relent."

"So I have been led to believe, sir; it is a characteristic of master-minds — no pun intended, sir—those sparks of humour flash out before one is aware. May I ask if you can tell me where Mr. Roland's bag is to be sent?"

"What bag?"

"His travelling-bag, sir; he brought no other luggage with him yesterday, and as he left it behind him at Morlands last night, I was afraid he might be inconvenienced in his toilet, sir. Shall I send it down to the Vicarage?"

"Take nothing upon yourself till you receive orders," replied Mr. Brudenell, more angry than he had felt for some time, at the significant sarcasm of the inquiry. "If your master is at home, be so good as to give him that," handing him a card, on which he had just written, "Dear H., I am coming to have a few words with you. J. B." "You will not forget, sir?" he added, with an emphasis that cowed the other at once.

"Certainly not, Mr. Brudenell; he shall have it immediately, sir," he replied, and seemed glad to pocket the card, and shuffle away, without the graceful swagger he had been rehearsing before.

Mr. Brudenell walked on to the cottage, and rapped at the door with his cane.

It was not often any one was at home, as the good woman worked in the fields, or went out charing or washing, wherever she could get a job; but to-day she was washing at home, and had to take her arms out of the tub, and wipe them on her apron, before she could admit her visitor. She was not alone, for her daughter, a pretty young girl at service in Durningham, had come over for a visit, and stood curtseying with pleasure at the sight of the Vicar. After a few kindly inquiries after the father, and how Susan liked her place at the Rectory, and whether she gave satisfaction to Miss Holmby—Mr. Brudenell came to the point, by asking quietly if Mr. Clarendon's servant were an old acquaintance?

"Oh no, sir, sure—it's not more nor a few weeks we've known him at all, is it, Sue? But he went over to the Rectory for Mr. Percival one day, and he and Sue got talking, and since then he has been several times, and when she's come over to see me—Miss Holmby she is very kind, and sends her over when she can, yes, sir, she do, with allus some'at for father, and a pot of jam or a basket of eggs for Mr. Percival—and if ever a dear young gentleman deserved the good things of this world, he do.

Dear heart, how beautiful he do talk, when one is all in knots, and can't lift hand or foot with the rheumatics—all about one's work, and one's dooty, till one is nigh upon mad to be up and about again, and can't stir!"

"You were speaking of Trail, Mrs. Smiles; does he often come and see you?"

"He come when our Sue comes, as I was a saying, sir, and of course, when I see that, I spoke to her and to him, didn't I, Sue? for, you know, she is our only one, and father he don't like to hear on it; he says as Mr. Trail was no good before the Squire took him on out of charity; but laws, he don't know half we do, do he, Sue? Fetch the pictur, dear, and show it to Mr. Brudenell; a real pictur, sir, that he is painting, his own self, of my girl; and though I say it, she is as good as a pictur to look at, and better too. That's it, Sue; bring it here. You hold it for Mr. Brudenell, 'cos my fingers is damp with the suds. Ain't it wonderful, sir?"

It was wonderful as a specimen of hard, staring, vulgar oil-painting, with just likeness enough to Susan's pretty features to make it the more detestable as a whole. Susan, as she held it up for the Vicar's inspection, little knew how terribly her own face told against the *chef-d'œuvre* for which she coveted applause.

"He is a clever fellow," said the Vicar, "and has an eye for a likeness, if he only knew what to do with it, and certainly shows good taste in the choice of a model. Thank you, Susan; let me put it down for you," and he took it courteously from her hands, and returned it to its former position against the wall. "You give him sittings here, I presume—not at Durningham?"

"Oh, not there, sir—Miss Holmby would be shocked."

"And you see a great deal of him, do you?"

"Not as much as they would like," put in the good-natured mother; "but young things in sarvice must bide, as I tell 'em, till they've put by a little to buy their bits of things decent. But Mr. Trail he says his wages is good now, and is to be raised, and he don't allus mean to be a sarvant neither; he speaks furrin languages, sir, and he repeats verses beautiful, quite like a print book, and he says Sue will live to be a lady yet, and he'll make her one, when she is his wife."

"Have you promised him, Susan?" asked the Vicar, kindly.

"No, sir," stammered Susan; "father don't like it; but then he don't know him, sir."

"Father don't like it at all, sir," added the

mother, "and he calls him a scamp. He made bold one day to speak to the young Squire, Mr. Roland, you know, sir, who got him a job at the wood-chopping afore he went away, and asked him about Mr. Trail's character—he was a groom then, you know, sir, and had just begun to court my Sue——"

"Well, what was Mr. Roland's opinion?"

"Mr. Roland, sir, he took his finger and thumb, just so, and snapped them, Smiles says, right in his face, and says he, 'My good fellow, his character is worth that, and he knows that I know it.' So father tells Sue he won't have it, and he likes Ned Bridges a deal better."

"Ned Bridges, the blacksmith's son? Ah, he is working with his father now, I hear. You used to be great allies, Susan, you and he."

"So they was, sir," said Mrs. Smiles, who gave Susan no chance of getting in her word—"so they was, and a good lad he is, and a shame it would be to say he warn't; but he can't paint a pictur, and he can't say verses, and he knows nothing of the furrin languages, do he, Sue? And he'll never make her a lady, poor lad, let him hammer away from morning till night."

"Hammering is thirsty work," said Mr. Brudenell. "I hope Ned does not drink."

"Oh, none o' the Bridges does—not one on 'em. They takes their mug, as you or I might do, begging your pardon, sir, but never more. They gets down a sight o' tea, though, for I see 'em myself—it goes in gallons, it do, when once they begins at it fairly."

"I wish Mr. Trail had the same taste in liquids that he has in models," quoth the Vicar. And he advised, with little hope of being heeded, that he should not be encouraged; told them what he knew of his old habits, and urged Susan to trust her father, and consult Mrs. Brudenell. It would have been lost labour to argue about possible ladyhood under such auspices, while her mother was at hand to keep up the dazzling delusion; so he wisely confined himself to one point at a time. The reference to Mrs. Brudenell was promised, not without some misgivings on Susan's part, and the Vicar took his way to Morlands.

Harcourt was expecting him, and the visitor was shown into the library, where he had been apparently engaged in sorting and destroying papers and letters. He looked flushed and feverish, and his hand was burning hot—no wonder, as the Vicar thought, when he was sitting in so warm a room, for the fire had grown furious with all the piles of paper thrown upon it, and the smell was rather stifling.

"Very kind of you to come, sir; take that arm-chair. I rather expected you, and did not like to be out of the way; so your card was a satisfaction. Where did you meet Claude Melnotte?"

The Vicar explained, and added, "I have to speak to you on that subject also. He is courting Susan Smiles, a nice, pretty girl, whom my wife recommended to Miss Holmby as housemaid. He has a wonderful tongue, it seems, and has turned her mother's head, if not hers. Now, as I am sure he still indulges in drink, this would be a sad business if it went on. She has a steady lad, much attached to her, who might have a better chance if your servant were out of the way."

"You want him out of the way, do you, sir? Well, I can accommodate you. I am going from home, and shall take him with me, and your young friends can marry meanwhile."

"Going from home—for long?"

"That does not follow; but I must run down and see my aunt before she begins her move, and Trail suits me better than many a steadier and more sober man. It sounds very discreditable, but the more you all cry him down, the more determined I am to hold him up. I do not require perfection; if he is sober in my presence, I ask no questions as to what happens behind my back."

"And if he personally offends you?"

"Oh, if he does that, like other people he must do it at his own risk. He knows the consequences, and will only have himself to thank for them."

The tone was not favourable to Mr. Brudenell's purpose, but he was accustomed to deal with human nature under trying circumstances, and was blessed with a larger amount of indulgence than most men.

"So you are really going away, Harcourt, are you?"

"Yes; what is the use of my staying at home? If there were anything worth remaining for, I would remain—as it is, the sooner I go, the better."

"I am sorry to hear you say so."

"I am much obliged to you for being sorry, and should be more so, if it did me any good."

"It should do you good to know you have friends who feel for you."

"Should it? If they would show their feeling, I might be more grateful."

"Come, Harcourt, you are a young man and I am an old one, and what we have to say should be said out openly; we need not be afraid to speak to each other on any subject, I think."

"I think differently; I am very much afraid of speaking to you on one subject. I am afraid I shall so speak that you will listen to me for the last time."

"No, my dear boy, you need not fear that. Your father's son would never forget himself so far; or, if he did," holding out his hand, "his father's old friend would forgive him."

Harcourt held the hand a moment, then withdrew his own.

"You know all that has passed, of course?"

"I do, and I am very sorry—how sorry I can hardly say—that my sister's child should be the innocent cause of your trouble. But, Harcourt, you must have known the truth—she never gave you any hope."

"Did that make it easier to bear? Hope? I had learned to believe—idiot that I was!—that I had only to stretch out my hand, and the bird would fly into my bosom. I found it was a lie, like everything Saville ever said, but it had done its work. We know who works by lies, and he is no journeyman at his trade. He has done a masterpiece, as far as I am concerned. Mr. Brudenell, you should not have come near me to-day. I am in a wild, rebellious, wicked mood, and nothing you can say will make me feel as you would have me. That boy is with you, I suppose?"

"He came this morning; he told us everything, and we had no right to forbid his telling Marion. And I am come to ask you plainly, if you mean, now he has begun to work independently, to make him independent?"

"You ask this, before consenting to his engagement?"

"Not exactly; after allowing him to declare his attachment, I can hardly prevent their being engaged heart and soul; but I ask it, that I may know, as Marion's protector, what she has to look to."

"Do you know on what terms Roland left me?"

"Yes; he feels aggrieved that you are his rival. Remember, he knows nothing of the circumstances, so honourable to yourself, which first led to your being so."

"No matter what he knows; I have as good a right to love her as he, or any other man. Because an impatient boy tells me of his fancy, which I know he may change in a month, am I to be forbidden to make my choice where he has made his? Could I go on as I did, thinking of her as my own, planning out a future that was to make her happy, and me in seeing her so, thinking that she was glad to be under my roof—glad to hear my voice—glad to feel the touch of my hand—could I go on with such a dream, and not make it a reality? I did not know how I loved her when I asked her in this house to be my wife—I only thought of her loving me. Now I know she does not care if I live or die, but I know also that, living or dying, I shall never care for any other woman—that I love her better than any one, or anything in the world—and that I will no more stand by to see her given to some one else, were he fifty times my brother, than I would have my purse wrenched from my left hand, while I had a stick in my right. You may go back, sir, and tell him so."

"Not yet, Harcourt," said Mr. Brudenell, with the calm dignity that disarmed insult by ignoring it; "I have not yet said all I have to say. We will pass over the question of right and wrong between you on that point. Are you aware how your father, the most honourable man either of us ever knew, came to make such a will as he did?"

"I do not know exactly; I always supposed he considered it his duty."

"The facts were these—it is time you knew them. Your great-grandfather so encumbered the property, that his son and heir was many years a poor man, and had not very long, by his prudence and economy, cleared the estate before he died. As it came to your father, he wished it to come to you, but justice required Roland should have his share, and he meant to lay by a sum for him every year. You remember your old relation, Mr. Eddowes, Roland's godfather. I was present when he announced to your father that he had made a will, bequeathing all his money to his godson."

"He said that, the old villain?"

"He said it, and I believe it was true. At any rate, your father did, and it decided him on leaving the whole of his property to you, as the eldest son. Mr. Eddowes, as we know, did not keep his word, or rather altered his mind, and left his money to the Alexanders, but your father did not know that in time to make a new arrangement."

"What do you mean by telling me all this now?"

"I mean, that there should be no mistake in your view of Roland's claims. Justice requires that he should have at least a portion of the inheritance, which, but for that mistake, we know he would have had."

"You are a bold man, Mr. Brudenell. What would the world say if I told them that my excellent and most religious clerical friend only told me my duty to my brother when his niece's interest became concerned in it? Would it not give a fine opportunity to those who are fond of throwing stones at church windows?"

"I dare say it might, and these plain truths are often as difficult to speak as a clever lie; but you know better, and that is enough. So long as you acted from love to the poor boy there was no need of pointing out your duty."

"And he sent you to make an arrangement with me, did he?"

"Not at all; he declares nothing shall make him accept a penny from you till you consent to his marriage. Unless I am much mistaken, he can be as self-willed as yourself."

"Well, Mr. Brudenell, I am much obliged to you for your openness, and I will think of what you have said. Tell me one thing first—do you approve of this engagement?"

"Yes—I love the boy, and I think he means to be steady. Percival has very good hopes of his religious principles."

"Should you have approved had I been her choice?"

"My dear fellow——"

"No hesitation, sir—I am in no mood for half measures. Out with it at once—you do not think me good enough?"

"I am afraid, Harcourt, all is not with your faith as I could wish."

"That is, I do not go to week-day service, and not always on Sunday—I cannot swallow Cecil Percival's theories, or allow my understanding to wear blinkers because my fathers tugged along in them without kicking. But you knew as much of me long ago, sir, and have not thought it necessary to give me up."

"I should never give you up, Harcourt; but I hope, if I live, to hear you speak of these things in a different manner. We will say no more now, and I will keep you no longer from your occupation."

He rose, and Clarendon mechanically did the same, but turned to stir the fire, and stood there as if not aware his visitor wished to take leave.

"She has been taught to think of me as one who believed in nothing—one who had no soul to care for what is good and pure. If it were so, should I care for her as I do? You have told me sometimes, when we have talked of such things, that there was nothing you would not do for me, to convince me your views were true. You have had conviction in your hands, and you withheld it. By Marion's side I must have gone in her path; for right or wrong, false or true, where she went, I should have been with her ; I had no wish to lead her in mine—but that chance, if it was one, is taken from me, and what the result will be remains to be seen. Are you going, sir ?"

"Why should I stay, Harcourt, if you have nothing to say that does not grieve me to the heart ?"

"Why, indeed? You have had enough of me for one morning, I should think. I wonder when I shall see you again."

"I will come whenever you send for me."

"That means, I am not to come to you."

"You had better not; your last visit gave very great distress, and now especially——"

"Now I am to leave Roland to his paradise. You are sure she loves him?"

"As sure as I am of her truth and sincerity. And Harcourt, I can tell you this, that she is very unhappy about this quarrel between you. If you have any real regard for her, you will consider her peace a little, if not your own."

"The quarrel is on Roland's side; if he will come to me, there will be one no longer. He spoke to me as I have never allowed any one to speak before, and never will again; if he does come back, therefore, it must be in a different humour. My doors are not shut—he has but to walk in at his pleasure; only he had better lose no time."

"He shall lose none that I can help," said the Vicar; "and now good-bye, my dear fellow, and forgive me if I have overstepped my privileges."

Harcourt nodded, touched his hand, and again stooped over the fire, but Mr. Brudenell, looking back from the door, saw that his head had sunk on his arms, and his shoulders were heaving convulsively. He strode across the room in a moment, and laid his hand on the young man's hair. "God bless you, keep you, direct you, Harcourt—teach you in His own time, and in His own way, even if it be by one which we are too blind to discover—too ignorant to know!"

There was no reply, nor did the Vicar seek one, but left him without another word.

"Roland," he said, the moment he saw him, "go and see your brother directly."

But Roland was obstinate, and would not go—not that day, at any rate, on such a message as Harcourt had sent. In the morning he changed his mind and went, and found his brother was gone.

CHAPTER IV.

MRS. LYNDSAY'S ADVICE.

A WEEK later, after her lover's return to London, Marion received two letters. One was from Harcourt, dated from Dover.

"When you receive this, dear Miss Egerton, I shall have left England, so you need not fear that I shall trouble you again. When I find I can approach you as a brother, I may venture to return. That time may be nearer than we suppose; every one tells me nothing is easier than to forget, and to change one's mind, and turn one's regard elsewhere; and popular belief is supposed to be true. I can only say it is no belief of mine, and I am used to be considered sceptical. I have been to see my aunt and cousin, and you may expect them soon as neighbours. Stella sides with Roland and with you, so you need have no secrets with her. She is a fine creature spoiled, and I shall not forget her kindness to me in this trouble. I am going to Rome, and may take a long tour, so shall not burden my correspondents; but I write to let you know that I have given instructions to my lawyer, whose address I enclose, to put himself in communication with Mr. Brudenell in the event of your marriage. Roland would not come and see me—perhaps it was as well. I was very near you both that evening. I prowled about your house for more than an hour—a pitiable object, no doubt, if you could have seen me, for envy and jealousy are not graceful ornaments, and my heart was gnawn by both. It is so still while I write, and I cannot consent to give you up, even though I know it will make little difference whether I do or not. God bless you, Marion, if I never see you again—perhaps the greatest blessing I could ask for you.

"H. C."

Through the tears caused by the first letter, it was difficult to decipher the smooth illegibility of the second. Stella wrote kindly, almost affectionately, congratulating Roland, and offering good wishes to herself; and at the same time, expressing sympathy for the pain the family estrangement must have caused. She hoped she had talked poor Harcourt into a more reasonable mood, and her cousin and friend might rely on her good offices in inducing him to do something for them both. She had encouraged him to go abroad, as the best chance of recovering his spirits, promising to look after his people at Morlands meanwhile; and they should lose no time in taking possession of the White House. Gervase Wray, who, by-the-bye, had engaged poor Mr. Saville's old servant as valet, had agreed to travel with him. Considering how sadly he was always out at elbows, you had no idea what a good fellow Gervase Wray was, when you wanted anything done. He had promised to let her know how Harcourt was, and give a general idea of his movements, and that was as much as they could hope for. A courteous message was added to Mr. Cecil Percival, and Stella was affectionately hers.

"She carries it off well," observed Mrs. Brudenell, to whom Marion read the letter. The same idea had occurred to herself; it was a relief to see that Miss Porchester took that frank, friendly tone, for she had rather dreaded a meeting. She was not sure that the writer meant all she said, but her having said it removed a great difficulty, and she did not hesitate to respond to the good will as she was expected to do. The Vicar, who had to go up to town to meet Mr. Saville on Marion's affairs, called on Harcourt's lawyer, to inquire into the arrangement referred to, but received no explanation—his instructions being to reserve it until the marriage of Miss Egerton.

The brothers had not met again, and Roland was hard at work in his office, and practising what he called rigid economy. As a preliminary step, he had sold out some hundreds of his small capital, and paid them into the hands of his brother's banker, for his immediate needs. Calling soon afterwards, he was informed that an account had already been opened there for him by Mr. Clarendon, who had placed five hundred pounds to his credit. Roland restrained himself before the civil cashier, but walked away, swelling with indignation. He would keep his word, he would not touch a penny of Harcourt's money—he would sweep a crossing first. Instead of sweeping a crossing, however, he changed his expensive lodging, which Gervase had left him to occupy alone, for a bedroom of much humbler pretensions—dined cheaply off the joint, in the middle of the day, with some of his fellow-clerks; and denied himself all the small luxuries of cabs, orchestra stalls, and such-like, which, now he had to pay for them out of his own pocket, alarmed him by their cost. Not a "run" did he get all that season, and it was an unusually favourable one; it required the comfort of Marion's letters three times a week, to keep this privation from pressing sorely on his spirits. At Christmas he got a few days' leave, and Mr. Percival would have mounted him, but his pride rebelled, and he declined. At Easter, which fell early, he tried for leave again, and failed, as his betters had to be served first; but by way of compensation, a branch of the Egertons, living in London, found out that they had a kinswoman still unknown, and wrote so pressingly to invite Marion for a visit, her uncle and aunt could not but persuade her to accept it. Roland was speedily introduced to these hospitable people, and requested to come whenever he pleased, which, he soon showed them, meant every day. Mrs. Lyndsay, hearing of this, came to make Marion's acquaintance also; and among them all Miss Egerton was in a fair way of seeing a little more of the world than she had hitherto done. The change was seasonable, for the White House had proved a poor substitute for Morlands, and notwithstanding all Stella's civilities, she could never feel that she was really her friend. Little things would come up unawares, that betrayed the existence of greater; and Marion's instinct, which rarely failed her, gave warnings she could not put aside and forget.

Her engagement to the man she dearly loved had met with slight obstacles in its formation, but it had been formed under circumstances nearly as trying as if it had been authoritatively deferred. It was not till this spring, removed from everything that could remind her of the calamity she had unwittingly caused, and exhilarated by the novelty and amusement of her cousins' mode of life, that she could be said, in any way, to realise the happiness of being loved. But even now it was disturbed by anxiety; her presence, instead of soothing Roland, seemed to unsettle him completely; he grew wild with impatience to make her his own, and keep her in London altogether. He pestered Mrs. Lyndsay with his confidences, till she told him she was afraid to see him come in; he besieged the General, he haunted Sir Perkin, talking them both nearly dead, but making them listen perforce—and at last fairly extracted a promise either of the secretaryship, the moment it should fall vacant, or of a rise, as soon as it was possible to give him one. How to get rid of the invalid secretary, who stuck to his post and his salary with a tenacity worthy of a better cause, was a difficulty; and Roland soon began to look upon him as an incarnation of selfishness, whom it would be a boon to society to remove at once. A feverish dread had taken hold upon him, that if his marriage were delayed, Harcourt would in some manner prevent its ever taking place. Every instance he had known of his obduracy of purpose, formerly either told as a good story, or fretted at as one frets at a passing grievance, assumed a threatening aspect now. That drive from the station, when he reminded him "he was master"—the sale of the horses, and dismissal of the groom, against Stella's petition, and his own—the favour into which he had taken the vagrant Trail, in opposition to the opinion of the whole house—these were all traits of the determination not to give up his own will, which was his brother's characteristic whenever he chose to exert that will at all. And if he had resolved, sooner or later, to defeat Roland's object, what chance should he have? He was beginning to think of Harcourt as an enemy lying in wait; and his nights were made wretched by alternations of feeling, from bitter regret for his lost affection, to equally bitter resentment for the manner in which he had been thrown off.

His cousin, Mrs. Lyndsay, was not long in discovering his state; and having made a few inquiries in other quarters, with her father's approval took upon herself to give Miss Egerton a little bold advice.

"Depend upon it, my dear, there are times and seasons, when a piece of imprudence, at the right moment, is the perfection of wisdom. We all know it is a foolish thing to marry on too small an income, as it is a very hazardous thing to take arsenic, or prussic acid—but as these sometimes effect a cure, when milder measures fail, so may that, judiciously applied. I am very impertinent, I am afraid; but even impertinence is not without its utility. I have seen a good deal of the world, and you have only seen a small corner of it, and I am convinced nothing is more dangerous for a young man like Roland, than to be left in London in this unsettled, restless, unhappy state. While you are always at hand, he is comparatively safe; but when he has that resource no longer, he will grow sick of his work, and crave excitement as a protection from unpleasant thoughts; and he is just the good-humoured, agreeable fellow who would be the soonest led into mischief. Take my advice, and marry him without delay, and make a wedding tour in Italy; and if you do not contrive to meet brother Harcourt, and win him over, you will not be the clever woman I take you for—in fact, you will hardly be a woman at all. Those two cannot be happy long apart, and they will never come together without help; they will both resist at first, and both bless you for ever, when you have reunited them. Think it well over when I am gone, and act accordingly."

Marion did think it over, and the result of her meditations was, that she wrote to Mrs. Brudenell, and laid the case before her. She had no fear of poverty—she was ready to economise and contrive, and do without anything they could not afford, if only Roland might be saved from temptation. She did not say from what bitter experience she had derived that dread, which rarely mingles with the plans of youth, but her uncle and aunt needed no such explanation. They knew all she meant, better, perhaps, than she intended they should; they talked the whole case over, with heavy hearts, but steadfast courage; they looked into their accounts, they drew up a balance-sheet of receipt and expenditure, and calculated to a nicety where retrenchment was possible, and where it was not; and at last Mrs. Brudenell made a proposal, to which, after considerable difficulty, she prevailed on her husband to consent. This was, that the three thousand pounds of which Marion had been robbed by her step-father, should be replaced out of the little fortune which the Vicar had with pains and toil accumulated by literary labour, and which, besides an insurance on his life, was all his wife would have to support her in the event of his death. It would come to her in the course of nature, as their adopted daughter, her aunt argued; and if she ever did want a home, Roland and Marion would give her one—she was not afraid. In short, she was so earnest, even to tears, that Julian could not hold out, and she was empowered to write back as follows:

"MY DARLING CHILD,—You are quite right, and we both love you the more for your openness and sincerity. Your uncle has a little plan, by which true love may be made to run a little smoother than it otherwise would, and when you have persuaded Roland to have you, he will write to him on the subject. Our one wish is for the happiness of our two children."

Whether Roland required much persuasion, may be left to be imagined. Mrs. Lyndsay waylaid him on his way from the office, and primed him to strike the iron while it was hot; promising, on her part, to do all that woman could, to induce Mr. Cromer, the inconvenient secretary, either to resign or die. Miss Egerton's relations were all for the marriage taking place as soon as possible, and from their house; and in Roland's present state of mind, a proposal that offered an escape from the sight of Morlands—from the spectral gap that Harcourt's absence must cause at the altar and at the feast—was almost as deep a cause for gratitude as the generosity of Mr. Brudenell, or the spirited interference of Florence Lyndsay. Marion saw it was so, and from her the wish passed on to her indulgent friends, and, as a matter of course, they gave up their own, and instead of a quiet wedding in their own church, among their own people, consented to the fatigue and expense of coming up to London. Miss Porchester was to be one of the bridesmaids—she took a lively interest in the whole proceeding, and between her and Mrs. Lyndsay, the bride was hardly allowed to have a voice in her own trousseau, except in the matter of expense. There they found she could be obstinate; and wisely refrained from wasting their influence. Leave of absence was obtained for Roland, and furnished apartments bespoken for the young pair on their return from their continental tour, the funds for which were General Alexander's wedding gift. They had private information from Stella as to Harcourt's whereabout, and were full of hope of a speedy reunion. Let them only find him, and it would not be their fault if they did not win him back.

"I have not touched a farthing of his money," said Roland; "there are his five hundred pounds, just as he left them. Till we have shaken hands, I should consider it a disgrace."

This was said the day before the marriage, before he had heard the settlements. He had been the first to insist, rather grandly, that Marion's fortune should be settled on herself; he was not prepared to be told by his own family lawyer, who attended on the occasion, that Harcourt had charged the Morlands estate with an annuity to Marion Egerton of three hundred a year for life, from the day of her marriage—payable in advance half yearly, and entirely at her own disposal.

"You will not touch it—you would not

wish to do so, Marion?" he asked, almost resentfully.

"Not till we bring him back to stay with us," was her reply. "We shall want it then, for he is nearly as particular as you are."

"You talk as if you were sure of finding him."

"I feel so; I shall never be happy till I have made him some amends. He might resist us separately, but we shall be too strong for him together."

Everything was settled, everything was ready. Percival came up to be present at the ceremony, looking more worn and hollow-eyed than ever; unable to keep away from Stella's side, and yet evidently suffering whenever he was there. That winter had been a torturing time for him, and the spring brought but little comfort. All the wisdom, and learning, and knowledge of human nature, of which he had been so proud, failed to teach him how to deal with the heart of such a woman; and he was, in fact, powerless in the light hands, that soothed one day and irritated another, and found solace in suspense and disappointment to herself by inflicting them on him. She had been ready and eager to abet his favourite schemes of musical reform and Church decoration—schemes which the Vicar allowed him to carry out, to his own apparent exclusion, though in fact, whatever was actually done, owed its success to his quiet support and judicious suggestions. Stella would lead chants and hymns, weave Christmas garlands, and illuminate Easter texts, or do anything in which she was able to be conspicuously useful and win a great deal of praise; but she would do nothing that was tiresome, and she soon showed she would not stand much contradiction—still less being lectured. It seemed to be a cruel pleasure to her, when the closed windows of Morlands were too gloomy to face, to see how she could force him to burden his conscience, either by breaking a rule, or deferring a duty, or conceding a point on which he had been stubborn before.

This was bad enough, but she had worse torments in store; for words of love had escaped his lips, and from that time she held him in a leash—and sometimes it felt like silk, and sometimes like links of iron. He could not really be a slave, but a captive he knew himself to be; and there were moments when he felt he must burst through every bond, and fly from her altogether;—and then a look, or a word, or an act of gentle penitence, would rivet his chains more firmly than ever, till it would have been easier to part with his life.

And now a step was going to be taken, which might end all by one blow. If Harcourt's reconciliation with his brother and his brother's wife should result in his return to his old allegiance, there would be nothing left for him but to go out as a missionary to the most ferocious savages known in the records of the S. P. G. If martyrdom ensued, so much the better; no one would lament him at home, and this weary struggle would be at an end.

This was not the mood for a wedding guest; but at that wedding sat many a secret care, hidden by festal robes. They made no outward sign. The Egertons, several of whom were light-hearted girls, were resolved that all should be as joyous as possible, and their high spirits prevented the thoughtfulness of the principals from being commented on. All passed well; the Vicar performed the ceremony, and Mr. Henry Egerton gave Marion away; the bridesmaids were faultless in dress and demeanour, and Miss Porchester was the object of general admiration, and by no means unconscious of the same. Roland was nervous, and Marion pale, but that was only natural under the circumstances. The breakfast was despatched with very little speech-making, as the newly-married pair were to start early for Folkestone; and the bride was just leaving the room to change her dress, when a messenger from the office brought Roland some letters.

"That is Gervase Wray's hand, I know," observed Stella, near whom he was standing; "and the seal is——"

She stopped short, looking at Roland in breathless dismay; he had torn the letter open, and was reading, devouring the words with eyes that seemed stiffening with horror. Instinctively his hands clutehed at the air for support—an attempt at a cry became a hollow, gurgling sound, and it was only Mr. Brudenell's rapid interposition that saved him from a heavy fall.

CHAPTER V.

A WALK THROUGH THE BLACK FOREST.

WE are again at Baden-Baden, and Harcourt Clarendon and Gervase Wray are sauntering together under the horse-chesnut trees, whose rich blossom betrays that it is unfashionably early in the season. There is hardly any stir in the place as yet—the booths are not half opened—the Promenade is desolate—the hotels are more than half empty—but the country is in its loveliest dress, and the inhabitants can enjoy that loveliness in peace and quiet, which is more than they can do later in the year. What perverse spirit of contradiction had driven his companion here now, Gervase could not fathom; his remonstrances had been thrown away, and to Baden he had come to in May, when there was nothing in the world to see but the beauty of nature. They had been here now two or three days, and Wray had contrived to exist, with the help of the table d'hôte, theatre, and écarté; and, being of a philosophic temperament, was contented to remain, so long as he had nothing to pay. He humoured his friend in every whim, and bore with his changing moods as no one else, perhaps, would have done, for it was no easy task. As they turned down the Allée on the present occasion, Harcourt suddenly stopped short. "I shall go a little way by myself now, Gervase; I will meet you again in an hour or two," he said, and struck off to the left, secure that his companion would not even wish to follow, when he saw where he was going.

There was another watching him, however, who had fewer scruples where he followed, to compass his ends; and as the young man entered the cemetery, a dark, stealthy figure was not many paces behind, though keeping back till a favourable opportunity should offer. Unconscious of being observed, Harcourt strode on, a little perplexed at first in finding what he sought, for changes are rapid in God's acre, and the army of crosses had moved an encampment farther since he saw them last. The keeper of the cemetery, however, helped him to recollect the spot, and pointed out the resting-place of Mr. Saville with some pride, as many English had asked to see it. His end had made quite a sensation; only, with a significant jerk of his thumb, one did not talk much about it down there. He had kept it tidy and clean, but there was no one in the place to give any orders, and to hang wreaths upon it now. Oh, the gentleman was too good—pocketing Harcourt's gratuity—and it should be under his special care, if he wished it. Perhaps he would like to gather a leaf as a souvenir of his dear friend?

"I have a more lasting one about me," was the Englishman's answer; and, when left to himself, he stood with his arms leaning on the iron rails, gazing down on the stone, with feelings against which it could ill protect the dead.

"And they are to be married," he thought, "and all will be over; and *he* must have known, when he told me that lie, what a lie it was. His man's evidence is conclusive; he played his last card, and played it well, and had he lived he might have won the stakes. I was a blind fool, ready to be deceived; and she, poor innocent child—what was she in his hands? She could no more have resisted his manœuvres for her establishment than for her ruin. And it has come to this, and he lies there, and no revenge of mine could touch him, if I would. Forgive him? Yes—I may come to that too, at last, when I have sunk down to his level; till then, all the misery he has caused be on his head—blasting him, even in the grave!"

"A fine evening, sir," said a voice, in tolerable English, as he walked back to the gate. "I thought I could not mistake the chivalrous friend of my poor George. You have shed a tear to his memory—he had many who mourned him, and I was one."

"So you were—I remember you now. Monsieur Le—Le—I beg your pardon."

"Lepelletier, sir. I am honoured by your remembrance. It is early for Baden; you are passing through, I presume."

"As I am through this gate; here to-day, and gone to-morrow, as our classic writer has expressed it. You are acquainted with the English classics, M. Lepelletier?"

"If I am? The immortal Williams, and *cette pauvre petite* Jane Eyre, and *les mystères de Londres*—ah, your literature is fine, ver fine, and your streets are full of melodrames that you have but to portray, and our blood freezes in our veins. I was in Londres once, once only—I shall never forget it. Dark, dark, all day long. Ah, it is a grand place to forge, and to work with steam, and to make money; but for *le plaisir*, there is no place like Paris, hein? Monsieur Clarendon knows Paris?"

"And the Parisians, M. Lepelletier; especially those we have the honour to meet in German watering-places."

"Monsieur is pleasant; I have the honour to wish him good evening."

And so they parted, and when, that evening, the friends went to the Opera, he was there soon after them, and wherever they walked next day he met them by accident. A strange whim seized Harcourt to encourage his advances, and try his strength with his own weapons; and, whether for the sake of excitement, or to provoke Gervase to remonstrate, invited him into their sitting-room, and let himself be persuaded to play a few rubbers of écarté, losing seventy or eighty francs in the course of the evening, the stakes being considered moderate. The next day, he sent for Lepelletier before twelve o'clock, and played with him again—played till dinner-time, and after dinner, till ten. The Frenchman's pockets, by this time, were beginning to feel rather comfortable; Gervase Wray was growing fidgety—Auguste kept him on the rack with stories of his old master's experience under this same professor. Going up to bed that night, Harcourt had some difficulty in obtaining the services of his *protégé*, Trail, and the moment he looked at him perceived he was not sober.

"What do you mean by this behaviour, sir?" he asked. "Have I not told you that you have all the rest of your time to indulge in your favourite iniquity, but that you must be without reproach when you appear before *me*?"

"I am as free from reproach as yourself," retorted Trail. "If the master gambles, the man may drink. *That* for your gentlemanly little virtues!" And, snapping his fingers in Clarendon's face, he found himself the next minute flying out into the passage.

No apology was offered next day; Trail was in a direful mood of sullen wrath, and Auguste warned Harcourt that he did not like his looks. Harcourt sent for him, told him, if he caught him drunk again, he should strip the coat off his back, have him pumped upon by the waiters, and sent off about his business; and not a word did he elicit in reply. That evening passed like the former, Harcourt losing nearly every game. Gervase began to grow desperate, and was sitting up later than usual, inditing a letter to Stella on the subject, when his friend came in, and threw himself on a chair by his side.

"Wray, I have had my fling, and tasted the pleasures of gambling, if that may be called such which is confined to losing your money. Now I am going to try something fresh. Get up at five to-morrow, and we will have a tramp through the Black Forest."

"Why at five?" asked Gervase, disconsolately.

"Because I am not going to bed, and that is as long as I can wait. Are you not in good training at present?"

"Not very; I am a little lame still." He had had a slight sprain a few weeks ago, and gladly seized upon its shelter.

"So you are, poor fellow—as lame as a tree when occasion serves you. Do you know why a tree is lame? Because it has but one leg, and that is a wooden one. Not bad, is it? Well, look here, by way of amendment, suppose we do this. I shall start at daybreak, with Claude Melnotte, in light marching order, and walk through the forest to Wildbad; and you can take a trap the next day, and join me there—dine and sleep, and come back the day after. Will that suit you?"

Anything suited Gervase Wray that kept

Harcourt amused without the assistance of Lepelletier; and the boon was cheaply purchased by the bore of a day's drive through nothing but scenery. He tore up his unfinished letter, and went to bed; and though his morning slumbers were broken by a good deal of shouting, and running, and ringing of bells, did not think it necessary to get up to wish his friend good-bye. Auguste reported, when he came in with his master's hot water, that Mr. Clarendon had gone off as he proposed, but that Trail was found so very hard to wake, having indulged in an extra cup overnight, that Monsieur, after raging and fuming for half an hour, declared he would not wait, and he must follow him. Monsieur would breakfast at Gernsbach, and Trail must join him there. Was the fellow gone? Oh yes—in such a temper! Auguste would be sorry, he vowed, to be at his mercy that morning. He had his master's pistols with him—he only hoped he would quarrel with no one on the road. The people of the hotel confirmed this account; they shrugged their shoulders as they spoke of the English valet—*un mauvais garnement*, as the head-waiter pronounced him to be, who had sworn at him for remonstrating at his calling for a quantity of brandy just before starting, besides having his flask filled for the journey. He would be in plenty of time for his master, as M. Lepelletier had gone also for a little excursion that morning, and had offered to carry him as far as Gernsbach in his carriage.

"He has gone on Harcourt's track," thought Gervase, more interested in this last piece of information than in the former, and he promised his friend no peace until he should have got him safely out of his reach. When the carriage came back in the afternoon without bringing Lepelletier, only a message that he might be absent one night, or two, Wray grew very uncomfortable. "Have a good pair of horses put to and at the door at eight, and mind you are ready," was his last order to Auguste before going to bed. He felt as if he should not be easy in his mind till he had seen Harcourt, and he was actually waiting to start before his conveyance was ready. The beauty of the drive was lost on him, and when he reached the hotel at Wildbad, where they were to meet, he eagerly inquired if an English gentleman and his servant had yet arrived. No English gentleman had come yet; but, as nobody was there, it was opined, anybody might arrive any minute. Gervase ordered dinner, looked at the rooms, lighted a cigar, and tried to be easy, but could not rest a moment. He sent Auguste out to reconnoitre; Auguste returned with a strange report that an English man-servant, answering Trail's description, had passed through the place—had been seen by several persons—had made inquiries about routes and distances, bought some provisions, and gone on, as he said, by his master's orders. How long was this ago? In the morning.

It sounded unlikely, and yet it made Wray uneasy. How that uneasiness increased when the night came on, without bringing any further intelligence of master or man, may be imagined. He did not attempt to go to bed, and as soon as it was day, called up the landlord, and explained his apprehensions, desiring that guides might be provided to accompany him in the search for his friend, to whom he had begun to fear some accident must have happened. Notice was also given to the local police, and a mounted gendarme sent off in pursuit of the individual who had passed through the previous morning.

The road by which the pedestrians were to have come was impassable in a carriage, and Gervase had to forget his sprain; indeed, anxiety would have driven it from his mind at any rate. A long, fatiguing walk it was to him, and for some time, without affording any clue to Harcourt's non-appearance. At last, a wood-cutter was found, who remembered seeing a man pass in the cap and coat, courier bag, and knapsack, with which Trail had started from Baden. He remembered it, because, when he had greeted the stranger, according to custom, instead of answering, he had thrown him a handful of kreutzers. Trail then had surely passed that way, but where had he left his master? On they went, inquiring of every peasant they met, until another man deposed to having seen two strangers yesterday whose description agreed with that of Harcourt and his servant, at the forester's lodge, a mile or two farther, where one of them was asking the nearest way to the Wild-See. He had heard the hostess describe the path, and believed the stranger took it. The servant, as he remembered that they all observed, seemed to be grumbling at having to go farther, and looked very sulky and savage; but his master only laughed at his laziness, and would not allow him to have more than one chopine of beer.

In return for this evidence, the man was pressed into their service at once, as additional guide; and with his help they at last found the path to one of those deep, dark, lonely mountain tarns, to which German fancy loves to attach the interest of legend and fairy fable, so rapidly disappearing even from these their favourite shrines. And here a trace was found again—a battered hat, and a mud-stained glove, both recognised as Harcourt Clarendon's. Traces of a struggle were discernible for several yards, where the soft soil was torn up as with the feet of wrestlers, and here and there were dark blood-stains, as if a wounded person had either walked, or been dragged along to the water's edge. And that was all; and when Gervase wrote, their utmost exertions had failed to discover anything more. He had offered large rewards—the police were on the track of the fugitive, and he could only wait now for Roland's assistance and authority.

He had not long to wait; as soon as steam could bring him, Roland arrived, accompanied by Percival and Harcourt's lawyer, having travelled without stopping or breaking his fast. The first stunning effect of the blow having passed, his grief and remorse could only find relief in the fierce energy with which he threw himself upon the track of the assassin. The calm, deliberate routine of German police in vain opposed its passive resistance; everything gave way before his passionate vehemence and profuse offers of reward, and the whole country rang with the tale of the murder, and versions of the supposed circumstances. The weather was very hot, and Roland was incessantly in the sun, resting neither night nor day, and heeding neither warning nor entreaty; and before his investigations had been productive of any result, he was prostrated with an illness that brought him to the brink of the grave. Marion had consented to remain behind when her presence might have been a hindrance, but at the first intimation of his danger she hastened to assume her rights; and he was often calling for her by name, unaware that she was by his side.

The search went on meanwhile; a certain amount of suspicion had attached itself to M. Lepelletier, who on his return to Baden at the time he had appointed, was at once apprehended for examination by the police. His statement, however, tallied with what had been previously ascertained. He had met Mr. Clarendon at Gernsbach, and breakfasted with him; and observed at the time that his servant was in a very sulky humour, increased by his master's ridicule—and the Frenchman had thought afterwards he would as soon have chosen Mephistopheles for a companion through the Black Forest. He had parted from them early in the day, and knew nothing more, nor could anything more be extracted from him. He was discharged accordingly, and quitted Baden, and the day he did so, the news was brought to the English party that a body had been discovered and conveyed to the town, which they were required to identify. Roland was then at the worst, so the painful task fell on Gervase and Percival. How painful it had been, Marion could read in their ghastly faces when they returned—faces that told her more than she had courage to ask, or they to speak of. Percival, indeed, could not speak at all, only wrung her hand, and hurried to his room, where he locked himself in for some hours; nor was it till after Gervase had given vent to more honest tears than he had shed for many a day, that he could give her any particulars.

Actual identification, he told her, had been impossible; the remains had been found partially consumed under a pile of half-charred logs, and the features were entirely obliterated, but proofs of the sad reality were not wanting. The body, stripped of its clothes, was swathed from head to foot in a large fine plaid of Harcourt's; and a seal ring had been found in its folds, which Gervase and Percival both recognised as constantly worn by their lost friend. The police seemed perfectly satisfied of the identity on hearing this—and no difficulty would be made about the interment. The whole thing, Mr. Wray confessed, had been too much for him—if it had not been for Percival, he could not have gone near the place; but Percival went through it all without flinching, being more used to such sad sights, and feeling them less at the time—however much they might tell on him afterwards.

A few mornings later there was another English funeral in Baden; and not very far from the monument of George Saville, was planted a cross bearing the name of Harcourt Clarendon of Morlands. Later in the day, a French Abbé, who had become slightly acquainted with the party from being at the same hotel, passing through the cemetery, saw Percival standing by the new-made grave in an attitude of such utter dejection, that he stopped to offer comfort, and say a few courteous words about the untimely fate of one so full of promise.

"It will not be offering an insult to your belief, I trust," he added, softly, "if I offer to remember him in my prayers."

Rather to his surprise, for a few sharp passes had already been exchanged between them on matters of belief, in which he had found the Englishman a ready master of fence, Percival grasped his hand in both his. "God reward you tenfold," he said, "for every prayer you put up to Him for the soul of Harcourt Clarendon!"

He turned to hide his emotion, and the kind-hearted Abbé felt it would be intrusive to remain. He passed on to leave the cemetery, but in so doing an impulse made him look back. The English clergyman was on his knees by the grave, and his face hidden in his hands.

"An interesting case, a very interesting case; plainly a convert to the truth, only waiting a gentle bidding to throw himself into our arms," thought the good man. "These English will be angels at last, if they will only lay aside their insular prejudices."

CHAPTER VI.

A NEW MASTER AT MORLANDS.

Two years had passed, and a third summer had just begun, and once more were the roses blooming in the cottage gardens of Stourbrooke, and perfuming the air that floated in at the open windows of the White House. At one of those windows is Stella seated, her work in her hand, though any one who had watched its progress would have found it as stationary as that of the Zegri lady in the song. As she lifts her face a moment, to listen for the twentieth time for an expected step, we may notice that it is altered for the worse since we saw it last. Her bloom is a little faded, and there is a weary, dissatisfied expression on her brow and lip, that is a fatal foe to beauty. Her thoughts, when alone, must have been but sorry company, for impatient gestures escaped her as if some irritating remark had just been made, and at last she gave up the pretence of occupation, and throwing aside her embroidery, leaned back in her chair with a long, restless sigh.

A step came at last, and she roused herself, with an assumption of cheerful indifference as her mother came in. "Well, mamma! I began to give you up altogether."

"Well you might, my dear; I really could not tear myself away sooner. The sweetest little baby you ever saw—quite took to me directly, and I had to rock her, and carry her about for nearly half an hour, till I was ready to drop, to stop her crying. The very picture of Roland, and, indeed, of Marion too, as I told them, and of course they were both delighted, and she is going on sweetly as she always does, let what will happen. I always do say she is the best-tempered young creature I ever came across, and I ought to be a judge, at my time of life."

"So you ought, mamma, and if she is not good tempered, with everything this world can give her, I do not know who should be. I dare say I could be as amiable myself under as favourable circumstances."

"So you are, my dear Stella—quite amiable

enough, I am sure, as you have not a husband and baby to care about, and a great place to look after, and all that. It really did me good, do you know, to see poor Roland look like himself again. I have not heard him laugh, as he did when I said the child was a picture of them both, for many a long day. I am sure I have talked and talked to his wife about it, till we have both agreed we could not bear to talk any more, and I quite despaired of his coming round at all, and said so—but this baby has put new life into him, and I am sure he was gratified by my seeing the likeness. Young fathers always are. I said I was afraid its being only a girl was a great disappointment, and he told me I ought to be ashamed of myself, considering my experience of what a daughter could be."

"Much he knew about the matter," said Stella, with a slight smile.

"No, very true; he could know nothing at all, but I thought it very pretty of him to say it, and indeed, I always say, no mother was ever more fortunate than I am, in having an only daughter, and being able to keep her so long. I used to think I should be left alone, years and years ago."

Miss Porchester had taken up her work again, and was stitching away in real earnest.

"Did you have a word with him on business, mamma?"

"No, really, I could not bring myself to talk about money, just when we were all so comfortable. It always makes me nervous to talk about money when I want it, and I thought I would wait, or leave it to you."

"We have waited a long time already, mamma."

"I know we have, my dear, and so have those tiresome people, by their own accounts, who are always teasing for their bills. I am sure I don't want to owe them anything if I could only pay them, and they go on worrying, just as if it was one's fault, and not one's misfortune. Stella, have you made up your mind yet about Gervase Wray's letter?"

"Not yet."

"Then, indeed, you must begin, for it is not using him well, and you must remember he is the worst hand in the world at making money go far, and while you are hesitating about it, he will be spending all his legacy, that might make you so comfortable. I do think it was very handsome of him to come forward directly he had anything to offer, even if it was not quite so much as you could wish. I always liked Gervase Wray, he is so good natured and civil; and I am sure I wish him well."

"So do I," said Stella.

"Then, my dear, why don't you accept him?"

"Perhaps for that very reason."

"Oh, if you are going to talk in that strange way, I have done. I never understand you in those odd humours. I only know we cannot go on much longer as we are now, and if you won't do anything to help us out of the difficulty, who will?"

"Do not be down-hearted, mamma; you may get rid of me yet, if that is what you want, but I must have time to think it over."

She took up a grey hat and feather from the sofa, and putting it on her head, went out into the little garden.

The noble woods of Morlands park, glorious in all their first verdure, had been the favourite object of view when she chose this house as a residence; since then they had long been a grievous eyesore, and yet she stood and gazed at them now, as if their fascination were irresistible. She thought of her past life, her ambition, her hopes, her expectations, all the energy she had expended in carrying her point with every one, and compassing her ends, as she felt she had a right to do—and what had been the result of all? That she was growing older, with fewer friends, fewer attractions, and the want of money pinching her in every direction. Their small income had never been sufficient for the expenditure she chose to think essential, and every year had only increased their difficulties, until they had become a very serious matter. Here they actually were, harassed by dressmakers, and upholsterers, and livery-stablemen, for their long-standing bills; and there—her heart sickened with envy, in spite of her better self—there lay Morlands stretched before her, with all its prosperity and wealth—and the possessor of all that she had looked on as her own, was her rival, Marion. How little she had dreamed of this when she saw her first, when she nursed her in her illness, when she took Roland's rose up to her room, really liking her well enough for a sister-in-law, and intending to be kind and patronising to her when she was. And she had aided and abetted her marriage, as the surest method of securing herself from the possibility of rivalship—and all for this, to find herself requiring help from Marion's husband, and to be debating whether prudence did not require her to become the wife of Gervase Wray.

"People may well say it is a vexatious and weary world," she sighed to herself, aloud. "I am sure I am quite tired of it, only I am not fit for a better, so I have to make the most of this."

A shadow fell across her path as the murmur escaped her lips, and she turned to greet Cecil Percival.

"Welcome back at last! I hope your holiday has done you good."

"Thank you; I hope so too. At any rate, my uncle's kind intention was the same." He took off his hat, and pushed the hair back from his forehead. He too was changed, and much more so than his companion. His eyes were sunken, and his cheeks transparent; and indeed his strength had so much failed that he had been compelled to give up pastoral duty, and nurse himself; and his uncle had insisted on his trying a continental journey, from which he had just returned.

"You have an inviting bench there, under the shade," he said; "may I sit down for a few minutes?"

They sat down together accordingly, Stella looking at Morlands, and Cecil at Stella.

"You have heard the terrible news," she began, gravely.

He trembled violently. "No—I have heard none—what? Where?"

"At Morlands—a girl, instead of a boy. Dear me, how I have frightened you. I really beg your pardon for my weak attempt at a joke; it was only because Roland was so eager for an heir, that he seemed to think the world would stand still without it."

"It is better as it is," said the curate, drawing a long breath, and trying to regain his composure.

"Of course we all know that, and he seems quite content. His cup is full to overflowing now."

"It seems so to us," said Cecil.

"Seems? It is. He has all he can wish for, and so has she. If one did not sometimes indulge in a little envy out loud, I think one would be tempted to do them a little mischief secretly."

"You envy them, then, Miss Porchester?"

"Now and then; at this present moment I consider my friend Mrs. Clarendon the happiest of mortals."

"Perhaps she is. Poor thing—she has had, I will not say enough of trouble, for that we know nothing about—but enough in her life to make her present happiness very sweet. Poor thing!"

"So you are going to pity her because she is happier than she was—what will you do for me?"

"Is that your case?"

"Exactly, only reversed. I am not at all happy, and I am in a great perplexity."

"Can I help you in it?"

"I do not know; I am afraid no one can help me. I have come to the painful conviction that I am a failure. Do not tell me I am mistaken, for I know you found it out long since."

His head drooped, and as he sat, clasping his hands absently round his knee, he seemed musing on her words.

"Failure—failure. Yes, it is the discipline of life, and it must be good for us, but it tries us as by fire. I know what it is, and can therefore feel for you, though I do not know how it is to be remedied. Failure, with every help, and every inducement, and such a prize in view, is only not hopeless because we are not alone. No, God be thanked, we are not alone!"

Her eyes turned on him inquiringly; his sadness had a degree of humility in its tone, which she had never observed before. And now she noticed that thin as he had always been, he was becoming emaciated, and streaks of premature silver were visible in his hair. Almost forgetting herself and her troubles, she asked, with some solicitude, if he were suffering in health more than usual? She feared he had been doing too much, busying himself for the good of others, and neglecting his own. Now he was come back he must take more care, for the sake of those who cared about him. And her looks implied more than her words, not unobserved by him, whose cheek flushed a moment, and then grew pale again.

"It is very kind of you to say so—very kind of any one to care for me," he replied, slowly and guardedly, "and I know it is my duty to do the best for myself, so as to have strength for my work. That is all I have to live for now, and for that I must try to live."

"It is not all you have to live for," she said, passionately; "no one has a right to say that who has made friends as you have, unless you consider they are to be thrown by when you are tired of them. If that is the case, I have nothing more to say."

"You know it is not," he said, calmly.

"I know nothing whatever, but that you have altered very much, and that one might as well look for sympathy from a stone wall. I had half a mind to ask for some advice on an affair that worries me, and which I should be glad to talk over with a disinterested friend."

"That is just what I am not," he said, rising in agitation. "I can never be disinterested where you are concerned; and the only advice

I should dare to give, would be that you should do what you felt to be right—right only. Never give up your peace of mind in the vain belief that it is required of you, either for yourself, or for another."

He touched her hand a moment, and was gone, leaving her in a tumult of feelings, which she could not, or durst not, attempt to analyse.

What his own were could only have been conjectured by any one who saw the look of patient anguish with which he pursued his way along the familiar road to his old parish of Durningham. Two years ago, he thought nothing of the walk, but it was a painful exertion now, and when he rang at the Rectory door, he was fain to lean against the wall for support. The maid who answered the summons was pretty Susan Smiles, who started and blushed at the sight of him, and was only deterred by shyness from stammering a welcome. He held out his hand kindly, and retained hers while he asked after her parents, and her health, and her comfort in service. All seemed to be as heart could wish; father and mother was purely, she thanked him, and missis very kind, and gave her a day out whenever she could. And how was Ned Bridges? Oh, he was quite well, she believed—she had not seen him for ever so long—not since Sunday, when he walked home with her—mother said he might, you know, sir, and father too—Mr. Clarendon was very good to Ned, and gave him plenty of work; he was saving a deal of money.

"I am glad to hear it, Susan. And you, too, are saving, I hope, and not spending everything as fast as you get it."

"Oh no, sir, I have three pounds in the savings-bank already, and missis says I ought to have ten before I—I—I mean——"

"Before you marry. No doubt she is right, but it cannot be done without self-denial, mind that. You have been very tenderly dealt with, Susan, and ought to be very grateful."

"Indeed, sir," her eyes flashing through tears, "I never would have cared for a wretch who could do such a thing as *he* did—I'd tear him in pieces if he ever came near me, and Ned knows it."

"He will not come near you, you need not fear," said the curate, after a little pause, "and we may leave him to his Judge, Susan. It is not for us to condemn our brother."

"But the Squire, sir, the master, who was so kind to everybody"—Susan was sobbing now unrestrainedly—"it was only that Michaelmas he had had the roof new thatched, and the floor mended, and everything made tight at father's, and not a penny of rent raised; sent them down a cock and two hens from his poultry-yard, because mother's had died off; and gave me a half-a-sovereign, his own self, when I went to service—so kind when he gave it, he made me cry. And to think that that wretch, whom he picked up in his rags, and every one here speaks ill on, should have been his death, and that I should be thought to have cared for him—oh! oh! oh!"

Susan could stand out no longer, and fled to finish her cry in the kitchen. The curate pressed his clenched hand to his heart; it was beating painfully and wearily, and he was sick and faint. He moved on to the parlour door, and very nearly stumbled into Miss Holmby's arms, who was just coming out.

"Dear heart alive, Mr. Cecil, and it is you! If I did not think it was Ned Bridges gossiping with Susan! You know she is allowed to see him at proper times, on condition he does not come without leave, and I was going to give them both such a dressing for breaking rules—and it was you all the time! How tired you look! Bless me, you have not grown a bit stouter for your holiday—no wonder, for I'll be bound you never tasted butcher's meat, at least what I should call meat, from the time you left England till the time you came back.

Wishy-washy soups, and cabbages, and garlic, and sour bread—I know all about it, and you are just starved. Well now, what will you take? We have a delicious ham in cut, and a cold pie, with savoury jelly, and Susan will put you down a chop in a minute—and by the time you have had your mouthful, the Rector will be in. He is gone to a vestry, and you know he will want something pleasant after that."

Percival smiled faintly, and yielded without resistance to the kind force that put him in possession of the easiest arm-chair; he made no protest against luncheon, and even took with avidity the glass of wine that was brought in as a preliminary step. His meekness almost alarmed his hospitable entertainer. She could not remember that he had ever accepted sherry at odd hours before, without the help of Brady and Tate. It was an opportunity not to be lost, and she slipped out to give orders for the immediate packing up of a goodly hamper, of which the cold pie and savoury jelly should form a part: and that the pony-carriage should be ready, when wanted, to take Mr. Percival back to Stourbrooke. A couple of chops were to be cooked instantly, not too much done, and brought in as hot as possible; and some new-laid eggs and freshly churned butter, put up to go with the hamper. Then she hurried back to her guest, who was leaning back in his chair with half-closed eyes.

"And now tell us all about it—what you have been doing with yourself, and what news you have brought. Did you hear anything of that miserable man?"

"Nothing."

"I dare say you inquired, though, when you were not looking at churches and paintings."

"I went for no other purpose; I found no object of equal interest; it was more to me than churches or paintings. Once I thought I was on his traces, but I never was."

"Are the police out there still on the look-out? The Rector says they wear all kinds of foolish uniforms; I should not have much opinion of a policeman in uniform."

"Even with that disadvantage," said he, with a faint smile, "the promised reward ensures their watchfulness. On the slightest clue being given, they will telegraph to the police in London, and from them we should hear directly—we may be sure of that."

"Well, I only wish it could be cleared up—not that I am of a bloodthirsty disposition, but for the sake of that dear Mr. Roland, whom I remember in petticoats, and a terrible pickle he used to be. It quite went to one's heart to see him so cut up, and if it had not been that his sweet little wife knew how to manage him, I don't know what would have been the end of it—I don't, indeed. I believe he still keeps all his poor brother's private rooms locked up, and lets no one but the housekeeper go in to dust and make them clean, and put everything back just as he left it. He can hardly bear to hear his name mentioned even now."

"I can understand that," said Cecil, shivering, as if with cold, in spite of the sunshine that streamed through the closed window. "I feel the same myself. Do not talk of him any more, there's a dear woman."

"Why, he was never a particular friend of yours, was he?"

"If he had been, I do not think I should have been alive now to answer you."

"It is as much as you are; I never saw any one so starved in all my days. You have never been well since you went up for the Clarendons' wedding, and had that journey at a moment's notice. Well, now they will be a bit more cheerful, and so, I hope, will you. Mrs. Clarendon is doing sweetly, I hear, and the little girl a perfect beauty. I went over to ask all about it of Mrs. Brudenell, and she told me it had come like a good angel to the house, bringing them a message of peace. Those were her very words, quite like a bit out of the Vicar's last sermon. There was no reason why they should reproach themselves, but they did, and though they were spending hundreds of pounds in doing good where their poor brother spent one, they seemed to think they had no right to be there, and were not worthy to stand in his room. You should hear your uncle talk of Roland Clarendon—he says he wishes there were a dozen such in the county, and he gives you the credit of a good deal. Now it is of no use for you to be shaking your head, and groaning for all the world like Aaron Brown, the Methodist class-leader; you know your uncle is not given to over-praising anybody—never said a flattering thing to me in my life—and he did think it better you should go to Stourbrooke, as you may remember. And he told me only last week that he thought the influence you had over young men was something wonderful, and that if Roland Clarendon turns out a higher specimen of the Christian gentleman than his brother, it will be greatly owing to his friendship with you. There, I won't vex you any more. Dear, dear, how poorly you do seem! I must just go and see if that mutton-chop is not ready; and if you would only condescend to take a short sleep meanwhile, it would do you twice as much good."

"Sleep!" murmured Cecil, as his well-meaning friend left him alone, "when shall I ever sleep quietly again, till I too am in my grave? O God, if I have done wrong, how can I now go back?"

It was, indeed, a summer-time of happiness that had come to the Hall and the Vicarage with Marion's little daughter, acknowledged by all authorities in both places to be such a daughter as no parents had ever been blessed with before. Nobody thought of regretting she was anything but what she was; her small self was the abridgment of all that was perfect in humanity, and the young mother, as in the tranquil days of convalescence she lay on her sofa watching Roland make his first essay in nursing—so anxious and painstaking, so proud of his own skill, so solemn and serious under his burden, until he happened to catch his wife's eye, when the old glad smile broke over both their faces—could hardly believe she had ever known what it was to have an aching heart. And yet her heart had ached sorely during those first years of wedded life. Even when all the long delays were over, and the proofs of Harcourt's death pronounced conclusive, and the inheritance his own, Roland had shrunk from returning to Morlands, and at his urgent desire they had travelled in the East, visiting scenes, to visit which had once appeared to Marion a dream of bliss. It would have been enjoyment now, the rather that change and variety were restoring her own spirits from the shock they had undergone; but Roland's restlessness prevented her ever feeling at peace, and wherever they went, his first object was to try and discover a trace of Robert Trail. He seldom named him to his wife, but to everybody else, guide or servant, consul or acquaintance, dragoman or fellow-traveller, she found he put the same inquiries sooner or later, and the faintest indication of a clue was enough to make him alter their whole route to pursue it—always in vain. This was stopped at last by Marion's strength giving way; and alarmed for his treasure, he yielded to her wishes to return to England. Once there, she soon won him to go to Morlands, and from that time, resolved he should remain, and if it were in human power, should be happy there. She devoted herself to please and cheer him, persuaded him to visit and invite his friends, to take up his old pursuits and sports, and, what was rather more difficult, to attend sedulously to his affairs, which the long interregnum had thrown into a little confusion. The result proved her wisdom, for occupation did more for his nerves and spirits than change of scene; she soon found that he threw himself zealously into his work, and took a keen interest in his people; and though the gnawing sorrow remained, it was paramount no longer. Under Percival's influence, who, ill as he was, still persisted in his duty, many reforms were made, and many rules proposed—so many, and so stringent, that it was fortunate for all parties when the expectation of applause led to their consulting Mr. Brudenell. His gentle hints and judicious amendments saved the household more vexation than they ever knew, or were, in consequence, ever grateful for; while in all that was really practical and good, he gave valuable support. And Roland, in his passionate love for his wife, and the full occupation of his time, found solace enough to keep his mind in a tolerably healthy tone. But, as his aunt said, he had never looked like himself till the advent of his small visitant, the sound of whose voice, albeit in anything but harmonious accents, gave him such a thrill of joy as he had learned to believe impossible. His laugh, even while limited to his eyes, was his wife's best restorative; and when he was handling his baby, and looking at her for praise, as Miss Porchester said, her cup was full.

Her recovery was rapid, and as she had grown somewhat wilful, especially with her aunt, who could refuse her nothing, she obtained more liberty at an early stage thereof, than Dr. Wartop would have allowed to a less petted patient. As she said herself, she gained her own way by not understanding any one else's, and as it agreed with her, nobody could find fault. It was more from prudence than from real weakness that she kept as much to her sofa as she did, and she claimed as much praise for it as Roland for his proficiency as nurse.

"I am sure she will be clever, Minnie," he observed, after a very careful examination of the infant features; "I am a great physiognomist, do you know, and I can see decided lines of intellect in the shape of her forehead."

"Can you, indeed? And yet they say she is like you, darling."

"Don't you be satirical. I am not going to have my daughter's morals corrupted by being brought up in French boarding-schools, where young women learn to be saucy to their betters. Seriously, now, Minnie, we must have her thoroughly well taught, and she cannot begin too soon."

"She is learning as fast as she can, I am sure. I never find her backward as far as her abilities go, the little darling. My dear Roland, you need not clutch her clothes so desperately; nurse says, no frock is ever fit to be seen after you have had her for five minutes."

"I will poison that nurse if she stands between me and my offspring. What are all these yards of stuff hung on to the poor little soul for, if not to hold by? You know a great deal about it, Mrs. Clarendon, you do, certainly. And whether you like it or not, my eldest daughter shall be a well-taught woman."

"I shall like it very much, dear, and you shall teach her yourself."

"Well, she might have a worse coach. Though I say it, none of the fellows passed better than I did, in that stiff Civil Service business; but I know even I found it hard work, from not having had it all driven into me sooner, so I am resolved Miss Clarendon shall not have to wait till she is four-and-twenty before she understands all about the Pragmatic Sanction. Here comes Aunt Brudenell, to tell me, as usual, that I am perfectly right."

"The right man in the right place," said Mrs. Brudenell, as she entered, and having kissed her niece, seated herself with her arms and lap ready. "I'll trouble you to hand over that baby, Roland, to its lawful possessor; there is Graves below, ready to tear his hair because he cannot catch his master, and sundry petitioners are waiting in the servants' hall. By-the-way, Cecil Percival is coming to see you, Marion, if he may. He wants to realise the pattern baby—or pretends he does—and if there is anything he wishes now, I am sure I should be the first to give it him, for he is looking very ill, notwithstanding his long rest."

"He should drink more wine; I'll send him in a lot of port," said Roland, "only I know he will be making half the old women in the place jolly with it, instead of himself. I wish he would marry—that is what he wants most."

"That is the best prescription you know, is it?"

"By far the best, only a great deal depends on how it is made up. Between ourselves, I am rather inclined to go and shake cousin Stella. She is breaking his heart."

"She would never marry him unless he had a handsome competence to offer her," said Mrs. Brudenell; "and even if he had, she would not like a quiet country parsonage. But shake her by all means, if you like. I have no wish to interfere in your family arrangements."

"No, on second thoughts, I shall leave that

to Minnie; it will be a safe outlet for her superfluous animation, which otherwise will be let off at my expense. I suppose I must go—as men must work, and women must monopolise the baby, but it is very hard that human destinies should be so unequally divided. I will soon be back, my little angel—shut up your eyes till there is something worth looking at; Minnie, she certainly will be clever—she minds what is said to her already."

"I wish you would do the same and go," said Mrs. Brudenell, "and shut the door after you. Clever, indeed, and a child of yours! Oh, my darling," as soon as the door was safely shut, "how much we have to be thankful for in this world—and what a comfort it is to see that boy himself again!"

"You never would believe he had such deep, tender feelings," said Marion, with glistening eyes; "no one did but I, and I only learned them by degrees. He would take all the blame to himself of every difference between them, even to those two unfortunate drives. He has told me over and over again, that if he had not been provoked into going out with Stella against his will, that man would never have got into John's place, and thence to the one he had. And yet we all know it was not his fault in the least."

"We will not talk of faults, dear; we all have our share of them, and must bear with other people's. The older we grow, the more charity we need, and the more we should practise. Teach that to this darling as soon as you please; she may wait for the Pragmatic Sanction a little longer."

And thereupon they fell into confidential discourse touching the small, all-important personage, who had by this time subsided into slumber, and were very happy over it, but said nothing necessary for their historian to relate, and were interrupted at last by the promised visit of Percival. His first introduction was rather a failure, as the baby, being unexpectedly awakened, expressed her disgust in a manner not to be mistaken or disguised, and was carried off by the nurse, exercising her lungs in a manner more conducive to her health, than to the harmony of her home.

"It is all the fault of your cadaverous cheeks, Percival," said the Vicar's wife, when she could be heard. "They are enough to frighten an old woman of ninety, let alone an innocent babe. I am tired of all this, I can tell you, and I shall now take you in hand myself. Miss Holmby came over almost crying because you were so thin, and you would tire yourself to death, going after all the old people in Durningham who chose to send for you—and forgetting your uncle, who was very much put out."

Cecil explained, that while he was at the Rectory, he had heard a poor old woman particularly wished to see him, and by the time he had paid his visit, he was too tired to pay another. He turned hesitatingly to Marion, almost beseechingly. "It was about her I wished to speak to Mrs. Clarendon."

"To me?" repeated Marion, who was now sitting up on the sofa, to show how strong she was; "is it a case for relief? I have done nothing yet, I am sorry to say, but Peters has a list, and she shall put her down. What is her name?"

He almost whispered it. "Trail."

Strong as Mrs. Clarendon chose to be considered, she could not control the blood that rushed to her heart at that fatal name, which no one ever mentioned if it could be avoided.

"Any relation——?" she was just able to ask.

"The only one remaining—his grandmother—old, feeble, and neglected. She helped to ruin him by her indulgence as a child, and by humouring him as a youth, and is not a model old woman by any means," he added, with a faint smile, "very dirty, and rather given to drink, as many are who have fallen in the world, and lost their self-respect with their respectability in the eyes of others. She has no claim but this—that she is his blood, and that all the world is therefore against her; the parish gives her bread, but no one gives her kindness. Her name is her curse—the very children avoid her—the kind-hearted women that sometimes do her a service, or give her a share of their meal, cannot help saying something that hurts her feelings. She had but one idol in the world, and after seeing it overthrown again and again, had just began to rejoice in its elevation, and to see others own it worthy her worship; you may imagine where her faith is now, and that it is no wonder if she be ready to curse God and die."

"Poor thing, poor thing!" said Marion, whose eyes were full of tears; "why did I not hear of this before?"

"She was not in such want at first; her grandson had given her money and presents, on which she had lived some time; but that is all gone, of course."

"What can I do for her? Do you know that there is a box full of that man's things in the house, which he had accumulated during the few months he was here. I had some difficulty in preventing Roland from having them all burnt, and I have often been afraid that he would. Ought they to be given up to this poor old woman, or have we no right to do so?"

"I cannot say; but if you wish, I will undertake the charge. Meanwhile, Mrs. Trail has earnestly begged to see Mrs. Clarendon. May I tell her she may?"

"Indeed you may do nothing of the kind," said Mrs. Brudenell, who knew by her niece's flitting colour how dismayed she was by this request; "you have no business to come talking about all this just now, and if it were not that you are young and ignorant, I should be very angry with you. A very little more, and nurse will be for putting you into the passage."

"I am young, and ignorant too," he replied, with no sign of irritability, "but I believe Mrs. Clarendon has nerve and strength to do what is right under any circumstances; I have done my duty in giving her the message—no, I have only half done it—I do implore you to see her as soon as you are equal to it, Mrs. Clarendon. You may live to be grateful to me for saying this; you may live to count her blessing a boon beyond price. Promise me you will try at least, and let me know when you can."

"I do promise," said Marion, moved by the indescribable earnestness of his pleading, "but promise in return, that she does not show herself to Roland. He cannot bear it yet, and I could not answer for what he might say or do."

"I will take care," he said, sighing, and rose to depart, followed by Mrs. Brudenell into the passage.

"I could shake you if I were not afraid of your falling to pieces," was her first observation. "Where is this poor old body to be found?"

"You will find her to-night at my lodgings. My landlady has agreed to let her have her back attic, and her husband's cart will fetch her over. She will not be there long—she is dying, and shall not die without such comfort as I can give. It is not much I have a right to offer, God forgive me."

"Well, you are a kind-hearted boy, with all your fads and fancies; and I can guess where Miss Holmby's good things will go. Only don't sit up at night, and I will come and look after your patient. It seems hard, indeed, to visit the sins of the children on the fathers, or grandmothers either, and yet we find it is so; th innocent bear the curse of the guilty."

Percival looked back nervously at the doo of the room he had left. "His angels ar watching there," he said; but there was a wild ness in his eye, as he said it, that was not i keeping with the trustfulness of the words.

CHAPTER VII.

AN UNEXPECTED VISITOR.

MRS. CLARENDON was sufficiently popular to make her happy recovery a matter of general satisfaction. Prosperity had not hardened her heart, or made her selfish; but her position had compelled her to judge and act for herself much more than by nature she would have been disposed to do. Her character had thus gradually developed itself, and in more than one instance had taken people by surprise. So gentle and yielding as she seemed on some occasions, they were not prepared to find her so prompt and decided on others; still less to see how her sunny good temper could be fired into active wrath by anything like deceit, overreaching, or oppression. Her servants learned this the first, and from the time that they *did* learn it, thought a great deal more of her than they did before; her poor neighbours and her school children were not long in discovering it also, and though it baffled some of their calculations, it heightened their respect for her authority. She was liked by her new acquaintance in the country, and the few intimate friends whom her husband possessed, either in the neighbourhood or elsewhere, for that innate good breeding, without which kindness of heart is of little real use in the world, and which supplied, in her case, the lack of experience in society. But they found she had a will of her own, and could assert it; and where she was convinced she was right, she would stand to her colours against anybody, or any number of bodies, with a spirit that delighted Roland.

It seemed to Marion, when she left her sick-room, and came again into the world, with renewed health and strength, rich in the blessings for which she had given thanks, as if her lot in life were blessed, not only far beyond her deserts, but beyond her powers of gratitude. In her own sphere she was paramount; her husband was even more devoted to her than her lover had been; she was the idol of the Vicarage—the queen of Stourbrooke, and the envy of Durningham; those who had been content with a curtsey, or smile of welcome, in the days when she first made their acquaintance by her aunt's side, would run out now to see her pony-carriage go by—fluttered and breathless if she only looked their way, and breathing admiration and awe behind her, as she vanished from their sight. She might teach what she pleased for Miss Poole now; that functionary was her most ardent worshipper, gifted with unlimited belief in her wisdom and erudition. Old Mr. Holmby paid her the most chivalrous deference, and conceded point after point to give her pleasure, for which both Houses of Convocation might have argued in vain—to say nothing of Cecil Percival. With the Squire she was a special favourite, and he would often ride over to chat with her about their respective dairies, and poultry-yards, and flower-gardens; teaching her a great deal that she was very glad to know, and thinking her all the more agreeable for being so eager to be taught. He would have been kind and attentive to her, as Mrs. Brudenell's intelligent, retiring niece; but as Mrs. Clarendon of Morlands, she was a sister potentate, and he pronounced her the most charming little woman he had ever met. And all this popularity being added to wealth and influence, it is not to be wondered at that she was an object of envy to

Stella, whom she now so completely overshadowed. Stella's feelings towards her, in fact, were beyond her own power to analyse. At times, she felt a strong yearning to win her affections and bestow hers in return, for there was that in Marion's nature which peculiarly attracted her own; at others, she could not keep down the jealous resentment that swelled her heart, as she thought of all her past visions, fulfilled in the person of a rival. At such moments, she could speak bitterly, she could frame cruel wishes, she could long to be doing something, equally bitter, equally cruel, that should bring Marion Clarendon down from her height, and reduce her to her proper level. Marion would find her, accordingly, sarcastic, indifferent, repelling; and would go away, slightly ruffled, saying to herself, that now she was quite determined, and nothing should induce her again to attempt a friendship with her husband's cousin. But the next time they met, Stella would have recovered her temper, and Mrs. Clarendon have forgotten her provocation.

On the whole, therefore, the intercourse between them had been of a sufficiently friendly character to pass for intimacy; and no attentions had ever been lacking on Roland's part to his aunt and cousin. Hardly a week passed without some good thing or other, from dairy or hothouse, kitchen-garden or poultry-yard, finding its way into the White House; not to mention game throughout the season, the loan of a horse for Stella, and the constant use of the carriage by Mrs. Porchester. The latter, indeed, owned in confidence, that she could not have been better cared for if Stella had filled Marion's place; perhaps not so well, for Stella hated the trouble of paying attentions, and would have been sure to want the carriage perpetually herself. If only the dear girl would marry, and settle comfortably, not far off, and if their income were only just double what it was, and everybody paid, she really did think she could pass the rest of her days at the White House, close to dear Marion and the baby, without a murmur.

Everybody paid—that was a serious clause, and growing so much more serious as days went by, that it brought Stella near the extremity she had long dreaded, almost with desperation. Gervase Wray was still kept uncertain of his fate, and knowing with whom he had to deal, waited patiently. Mrs. Porchester's heart failed her every time she had been sent to talk to her nephew on money matters; and Stella found it would be easier to speak to his wife first, than to face her afterwards.

They were sitting together in Marion's morning-room, the sweet scent of haymaking coming in at the open window, Nelson lying at Marion's feet, who, with a small note-book on her knee, was putting down names as they occurred to herself or her companion. The baby had, of course, been christened as soon as she could take it to church; but the proposed *fête* in its honour had been deferred till her complete recovery. It was now a decided point that it was to be given as soon as the hay was saved, and Stella, as possessing the experience in which Mrs. Clarendon was deficient, was her prime counsellor in her difficulties. All was amicably settled at last—the arrangements for croquet, the band of music, the collation, and the dancing; and the list of guests only waited for Roland's sanction and additions. It was to be partly a juvenile *fête*, as appropriate to the occasion, and Mr. Brudenell's friends, the Grahams, were to sleep at the Vicarage the night before, that the three little girls might share the unwonted treat. General Alexander and Mrs. Lyndsay, with other guests from a distance, would be accommodated at Morlands, and Marion suggested inviting Mr. Wray.

"Gervase Wray?" said Stella, quickly; "then I shall stay at home."

"My dear Stella, I beg your pardon; I only named him because I thought it would be just what you would wish."

"I wish sometimes that I had never seen his face; at others, I am tempted to see too much of it. Ah, Marion, you are a happy woman!"

"So I am—much happier than I deserve, or than I once thought I ever could be. I should be happier still if I could help to make you so. What is it?"

And she pushed her memoranda away, and looked earnestly at her visitor. Stella had learned the language of that look: she knew what it was saying now. "Tell me the truth, and only the truth, for I am sure to find it out if you don't." More than once had she drawn back from an intended evasion, sooner than meet it—more than once, having met, she had yielded to the spell of sincerity, and opened her soul without reserve. That spell wrought on her now.

"It is just this," she said, "that my mother and I have so much exceeded our income, that we must do something to retrieve our affairs, and Gervase Wray will accommodate my mother, if I will consent to marry him. Just like him, is it not? You know he has realised one of his numerous 'Great Expectations,' and has more money to spend than he ever had before; so the first thing he does in the way of investment is to offer to buy *me*."

"You do not love him?"

"Love him? No—his bargain would be a good one, if he could have love for his money. But I am tempted to close it, notwithstanding."

"You would be miserable, Stella."

"Not more so than others—not more so than I often am now. You would be afraid of me if you knew half the wicked things of which I feel capable sometimes."

"I dare say I should; but you will never do them. Stella, I wish I knew the real state of your heart. I have thought more than once that I understood you, but I am uncertain still. If I knew the truth, I should see my way clearer towards helping you."

"Tell me what you conjecture, and I promise to answer truly—and, moreover, not to be affronted, which I see you expect will be the result."

"On that promise, then, I will rely. I have thought, often thought, that the man you really love—have loved all along—is Mr. Percival."

There was a short silence before Stella replied, "I have often thought so too."

"I was sure of it—and he is so good, and

looks so unhappy, and I do believe it is all your fault."

"His goodness, or his unhappiness? Depend upon it, my dear, the one is the cause of the other, and not any cruelty of mine. He has dreams of impossible perfection, that must be attained by making yourself perfectly miserable and odious, and it is killing him, as everybody may see—but it is not my doing. He could stay away the whole winter, and come back cool and indifferent; and if that be love, I would rather have nothing to say to it."

"But if his apparent indifference only means that he does not think you care for him, or that he has not a fortune to offer you—would it not add to your happiness if these hindrances were taken out of his way?"

"I do not know—it might. I have had my dreams too; but I am afraid he would expect too much from me. I am not good enough for him, and if he does not think so now, he would then. Marion, do you remember that day I was your nurse—the day after your accident?"

"I am rather confused about those days, but I do remember your sitting with me, and bringing me a rose from Roland."

"Did you overhear anything that was said that day by the maids in the next room?"

"I did, but I was never sure that I had heard rightly, and it confused my head all night. I had a vague, wretched feeling that I had done something to injure you, and that you were hating me for it; and it haunted me (I do not mind owning it now) till I had seen you again, and found you as kind as ever."

"If I was kind, it was because I was too proud to be otherwise; but, Marion, many a time during that period I could have rushed into your room, and told you I hated you. It rankled in my temper till it became unbearable, and I revenged myself on Harcourt by encouraging Mr. Percival. I know it was very wrong, for my motives were as low as they could be, and I am punished for all now. A few years more, and I shall be out of fashion, and pushed aside by my juniors, and have nothing to look forward to but green tea and gossip, if I can afford to buy the one, or find any one to indulge me in the other."

She had risen, and walked to the window in suppressed excitement.

"I trifled with two such hearts as I shall never meet with again. Harcourt loved me then, better than you; those women were only repeating the idle slanders of the servants' hall: he did love me, I know, and thought no one my equal—but I vexed and thwarted and irritated him, and let him think I preferred another. And that other loved me too, and believed he was winning me, when I was using his regard as the tool of my jealousy and pride. Now it is his turn, and I must bear what I deserve—and I suppose it will end in my marrying Gervase Wray."

"That it shall not," said Marion, "if I can prevent it. You shall not throw your happiness away for want of a little help." And she followed Stella to the window, and passed her arm round her waist. "Look upon us as your brother and sister, and let us act for you. I am to see Mr. Percival presently, as I promised to call on that poor old woman to whom he is so kind. When I went before, she was asleep, and I would not have her disturbed. And for the rest, Stella, I must talk to Roland, and see what he says. I am quite sure he would do anything he could, and so would I."

These were simple words, but of their sincerity there could be no question, and Miss Porchester's heart felt relieved of half its burden. Her own unwonted humility gave her a sense of peace and rest that were strangely refreshing; and jealousy and envy were laid to sleep. If indeed Cecil loved her still, and she could begin a new unembarrassed life under his guidance, the gnawing vacuity would be filled up, and the disappointing past remembered only as a dream. And during the rest of the day she was weaving plans of rapid clerical advancement, by which he would be able both to distinguish himself, and to place her in the position in which she felt she should do him most credit. He was a bishop, at least, before she fell asleep that night, and the newspapers were full of reports of the last great speech by which he had electrified the House of Lords.

Marion, meanwhile, had paid her promised visit, which, the longer it was delayed, only made her the more anxious to get it over. She meant it to be her first and last; shrinking, as every one did, from the very name the old woman bore, and having done what was required, to make Percival her almoner afterwards. The room was clean and tidy—Cecil's landlady took care of that, and her daughter attended to the poor creature's little wants. She had taken to her bed as soon as she arrived, and there seemed little probability of her leaving it. Unattractive, common-place she was in every respect, but her heart was breaking, and her only comfort was in the presence of Mr. Percival. He had surrounded her with remembrances of her grandson. His paintings, rescued secretly from destruction at Morlands, hung on the wall; his box of clothes was in a corner—an old book of plays he had pawned at Durningham was on the table near the bed, by a Bible and Prayer-book. Not that she read either, for except when Cecil was by her side, her intellect seemed to be in a half torpid state. She would lie and mutter to herself, Mrs. Andrews told Marion, for an hour together, and sometimes cry about her poor boy; but she never talked to any one but Mr. Percival, or seemed to care about anything that any one else said to her. She hardly noticed Mrs. Clarendon, until the curate came in, and bending down to her ear, repeated the name distinctly. Then her glassy eyes lighted up for a moment, and she half whispered, with eager exultation, "They telled me he saved her life—she'd ha' been smashed to bits if he hadn't laid hold on them beasts, like a brave lad as he allus was. He promised me a new red cloak come Christmas, but he went away without giving it, and I shan't have it now. He'll not come back no more, no more—he allus said he should do better in another country, and I'll be bound he has. Got a home of his own, and forgets his granny altogether."

And she whimpered a little, and went on muttering.

"Her mind is going," said Marion, in a low voice to Percival, whose look of intense anguish she could not understand. Her own feeling was that of pity, so mixed with horror and aversion, that she would gladly have put her purse on the table, and escaped from the house; but his quiet, authoritative sign, as he took a small book from his pocket, compelled her to remain.

"I am going to pray with you, Mrs. Trail," he said, very gently.

"Ay ?" was her only answer.

"I am going to ask God to have mercy on a poor wanderer, heavy-laden with guilt, and needing the prayers of his brethren, especially those he has wronged. Will you join with me ?"

She was evidently accustomed to such an appeal.

"Ay, God bless him, wherever he is !"

"Amen !"

So fervently and solemnly was this uttered, that Marion looked at him in astonishment; and saw that he was watching her with eyes full of tears. He knelt down immediately, and she could do no less; and before the short prayer was ended, she was almost weeping too. Whether the old woman followed his words, they could not tell; but when they had risen from their knees, she looked round almost cheerfully.

"He'll sleep the better for that, and so shall I. Good-bye, my dear—God bless you."

"Shake hands with her," said Percival, and Marion felt compelled to obey. He went with her to the door, and gave her his arm down stairs. "Thank you," he said at parting; "you have set us all a good example; you have obeyed in simple faith, not asking a reason. And though you do not know it, you have your reward."

She had another reward, for which she was not quite prepared. Roland was at home when she returned, and asked where she had been. She explained, as tenderly as she could; but for the first time in his life, he was angry with her. He wondered she could have done such a thing—have offered him such an affront:—Percival ought to be ashamed of himself for asking it—it must not happen again. The workhouse was the place for the woman, instead of sentimental coddling under their very eyes, at the gates of their very house. "How could you do it, Marion?" was his last reproach, as he strode away to his dressing-room, and locked himself in. It was a terrible discovery to her that she could so grievously offend him, and the moment he appeared again she was ready with a petition for forgiveness. She would not shield herself by laying the blame on Percival, neither could she say she thought she had done wrong; but that Roland was displeased was misery enough, and she was more anxious for pardon than for acquittal. Happily for both, his anger was never long-lived, and the moment he saw her distressed, he pronounced himself a brute, undeserving of such an angel; but angel as she was, she must discriminate in her visits; and if she did not wish to give him pain, must leave Percival's *protégée* alone. She acquiesced with perfect submission, and, with wifely tact, decided on not bringing forward Stella's case till the next day.

The next day brought its own cares; urgent letters from London demanded Roland's presence on matters of business, likely to detain him till the arrival of his guests, unless he started immediately; and start he did, promising to despatch matters as quickly as he could, and giving her carte-blanche, meanwhile, in all arrangements—as, indeed, she generally had. The subject of Widow Trail was not revived, but Marion put money into the hands of her uncle, and felt her conscience clear towards all parties. She could not even wish to see again a person who had brought upon her the only unloving look she had ever met from her husband's eyes—a look that would return, long after Roland had forgotten it.

If tender letters could have made her forget it, too, she received her share; but his business was not so readily despatched as he expected, and day after day slipped by without bringing him back. He faithfully promised to be home in time for General Alexander, who was to arrive the day before the *fête;* but that very morning came a few scrawled, blotted lines, as if written in violent haste, telling her news had come to the police from Germany, which made it necessary for him to start by the night mail; she must make his excuses—his friends would feel for him—he would write when he could. And Mrs. Brudenell, coming over to see what help she could give, found the lady of Morlands very much disposed to cry over this disappointment.

"Dear child," she said, briskly, "may you never have a heavier care! The poor boy was right to go, if anything has really come to light, and if he had been prevented, would have made himself ill, as you know. It is hard upon you, but you must show you are equal to an emergency, and don't give good-natured people anything to talk about."

Marion admitted this was good advice, but her heart being full, she confided the fact which oppressed her, of having made him angry the day before he left.

"Is that all you are fretting your little heart about? When you have done it a dozen times, you will think nothing of it. I tell you what, my darling, it is not pleasant to see a man cross, but then you can have the consolation of thinking how much better you are than he is; it is living with a husband like your uncle that is the real trial—a man who is always right; and to whom you are obliged, sooner or later, to own that you are wrong. So make yourself easy with this reflection, that bad as your case may be, it will never be so bad as mine."

"A person wishes to speak to you, ma'am."

The words were dropped in Marion's ear as the butler took her coffee-cup that evening. She had followed her aunt's advice, and exerted herself diligently for the entertainment of her guests, and, supported by Stella, and encouraged by Mrs. Lyndsay, had gone through her part with considerable success. Courteous allowance was made for Roland's absence, and due sympathy expressed for the cause; and the General took the bottom of the table, and was now keeping Mr. Percival of Durningham well amused by political anecdotes, over their wine. Cecil had been invited, but declined on the plea of business; and the first idea that crossed Mrs. Clarendon's mind, on hearing that she was wanted, was that it was some message about old Mrs. Trail.

"What person is it, Richards, do you know?"

"No one belonging to this place, ma'am, I think. He speaks like a foreigner, and I should say, he was just off a journey."

"Go and ask his name, and what he has come about, as I am engaged to-night. If it is only to ask for money, let him call in the morning."

"Yes, ma'am." Richards collected the cups, and withdrew; but presently returned, with a slip of folded paper on his salver. "If you please, ma'am, he gave me this to deliver to you."

The other ladies looked on curiously, as Marion opened the paper. It only contained these words, in a scarcely legible hand. "My business, Madame, is secret, urgent, most important. Deign to accord a few minutes to an old friend of the late Mr. Saville."

"Where is the person, Richards?" she asked, as she twisted up the note in her trembling fingers.

" He is in the hall, ma'am."

" Put lights in the library, and show him in there. Stella," as her cousin came up with an inquiring glance, " will you show Mrs. Lyndsay the cameos we were talking of at dinner? They are in that cabinet; I am wanted by somebody. I shall be back in a minute."

She hurried to the library; the name of her step-father being quite enough to fill her with a nervous dread of any one but herself hearing what there was to be told.

" Wait in the hall, Richards," she said to her stately retainer, as he opened the library door to let her pass; and the next moment she was alone, with a tall, foreign-looking personage, in green spectacles, who bowed as she entered, with an apology, in tolerable English, for his unseasonable intrusion. He feared he had not the honour of being remembered by Madame; it was long since they had met, but he believed she would know the name of Achille Lepelletier. That name was indeed sufficient, and when he removed his spectacles, she remembered him only too well.

" I am at a loss to imagine, sir, what you can have to say to me," she began, with some hauteur, " or why you have described yourself to me as Mr. Saville's friend."

" Pardon me, Madame, that last presumption; it was my knowledge of your tenderness towards that deceased gentleman that made me foresee you would not resist an appeal to his memory. I have not deceived you, Madame," seeing her about to move to the door, "my business is all I have described to you—and more. I will not detain you long—permit me first to offer my humble and respectful congratulations on your brilliant lot. Our deceased friend would indeed rejoice in his tomb if he saw what I see to-night."

She knew what was in his mind; she knew how differently she was dressed now from the time when she had first seen him, in her mother's presence, on one of those occasions, never to be obliterated from her memory, when Mr. Saville, pushed to extremity, had called on his wife for aid, and, by solemn vows of amendment, wrung from her almost the last remnant of her husband's wealth. The whole scene passed before her, and she could with difficulty retain composure enough to request he would state his errand as briefly as possible, as she was particularly engaged.

"I will be brief, Madame, if you will be patient. Are you aware that the evening of Mr. Saville's lamented decease he borrowed of me a sum of money, which was not repaid?"

"No, sir; I have heard nothing about it;

and I do not see that it concerns me in the least."

"Consider, Madame, consider. You were as his daughter—you revere his memory—you would not wish a stain to rest on his honour—and why was this money borrowed? It was to play—to play at the tables; and with that money of mine he did play and he did win hundreds, and it killed him, and I was too tender-hearted, too sorry for you, *pauvre demoiselle*, left so suddenly, to press my claim: *mais enfin!* I am poor, I want money, I come to see if you are generous, and will pay me back what is my due."

"I can undertake nothing of the kind without Mr. Clarendon's sanction, and he is not at home. If you choose to state your claim in writing, and send it to me, I will show it to him on his return. And now I shall wish you good evening."

"Stay, Madame; you have not heard all yet—this was only a little beginning—I have more to say. Listen, Madame, for what I tell you concerns you, your husband, your young child—all your house. It concerns not me, but as business—to you it is life and death. You listen?"

She bowed coldly, for she was as yet incredulous.

"Ah! you do not believe—wait! I have a family secret in my power—a terrible secret—and no one knows it but me, and I am come to sell it to you. Your husband is away—I know it: I know more—he is out of England. I cannot wait till his return. I come to you, his wife: you hold his purse—you can buy. One hundred pounds for my secret, and it is yours, and if you like to tell it, that regards *you*—if you would bind me to tell no one else, one hundred pounds more, and I am silent for ever. Fifty pounds I lent Mr. Saville—two hundred and fifty in all. You will buy?"

"Certainly not: I can have nothing to say to such a proposal without knowing more."

"Ah, but you cannot know till you buy, and when you buy, then you open your purse, and fold your hands to make me silent. You do not know—you are a child, playing at the foot of Vésuve, and the liquid fire will pour over you while the toys are in your hands. I offer you escape, and you hesitate. Why should I come here to-night, if I had nothing to sell? In England no man gives anything—all is bought and sold, even your national honour—bah! I offer you to-night—to-morrow, if I do not sell to you, I offer to others—they will not pay me to be silent, but to speak—

that suit you not so well. You love your husband, your child; you can save them—will you buy?"

Marion put her hand to her forehead; his earnestness impressed her, in spite of her contempt. Was it possible that he was speaking the truth—that he could have anything to reveal that could affect Roland, or her little one? It seemed too monstrous to believe, and yet a sickening fear of she knew not what seemed creeping through every vein. He saw his advantage, and pursued it.

"Remember this, Madame, I warn you against asking advice. To me it matters not, but to you it matters greatly. You will wish you had paid double, before you let any one know what I have told you. I swear I am speaking the truth—and I know you are beginning to believe me."

"I do believe you are in earnest, sir; though it seems impossible that you should not be mistaken. But you must be aware I do not keep such sums of money in the house—I must have time to think it over, and if I decide on giving what you ask, you shall have it as soon as it can be procured. I say this without making any promise; and now I must beg you to leave me. What is your address?"

"Madame, I will call again to-morrow at noon, to learn your pleasure. I am quite safe in your house—you are a lady, and honourable, and would take no mean advantage of my confidence. You will allow me a crust of bread before I go: I have travelled far, and am hungry."

She opened the door, and called Richards.

"Bring a glass of sherry and some biscuits."

The butler hastened to obey, and Lepelletier, with a low bow, drank the wine, pocketed the biscuits, and turned to depart. "To-morrow, at noon, I shall do myself the honour. Adieu, Madame, adieu!"

He was gone, and Marion went back to her friends, turned off their inquiries as lightly as she could, conversed, played and sang, and did her duty, with throbbing pulse and burning cheeks, that impressed Mrs. Porchester with the dismal conviction that she would be ill the next day, and the party put off. "The first real party she has ever given here, it would be so extremely unlucky for her to be ill," she repeated so often, that Mrs. Lyndsay replied at last, she thought it might be equally unlucky if it were the twentieth. And Marion, overhearing them, laughed, as at some excellent joke, denied that she was ill, and went across the room to be talked to by old Mr.

Percival, about the comparative size of the timber of Durningham and Morlands.

"I ask no impertinent questions, Marion," were Stella's parting words, "but if there is anything we ought to know, let us know it soon. When will Roland come back?"

"I shall have a letter some time to-morrow. Don't talk of it—I can hardly bear it as it is," said Marion, with a sob, as she turned hastily away to help Mrs. Porchester with her cloak.

The house had been still an hour, and yet she had not undressed. Her maid had taken the flowers from her hair, and had then been dismissed to bed. She wanted to be alone, to think quietly over the strange interview of the evening, and decide what she ought to do. As she sat musing, and weighing probabilities, she suddenly recollected the packet of money delivered to her by Harcourt, and which, at her request, he locked up again in his desk. She remembered his telling her there was a memorandum of the amount, and of a debt to Lepelletier—she thought he said it had been paid. The desk was still where he left it, in his private room, where no one ever went but herself and Peters, to see that all was kept in order. The keys were in her possession; Peters was gone to bed by this time, but there was no reason why she should not go into them alone. She took a candle, and having ascertained that there was no chance of being seen, unlocked the door of the private staircase by which she had been brought by Peters the first time she visited those deserted apartments.

She had not quite realised how lonely they would look at that hour, by that feeble light —nor the force with which the memories of that first visit would rush upon her mind. As she stood in the little workshop, with Harcourt's carving on the walls, his tools, his lathe, his pile of wood in the corner where he left it,—and put into the lock of the desk the little Bramah key she remembered so well, it seemed as if it were only yesterday that she had come in there as his guest, and had seen him open that outer door—never opened since he went away. And she thought how tenderly and kindly he had spoken—how considerate he had been of her feelings—how generous in all his dealings with her and hers—and heavily did it strike on her heart, that it was she who had been the innocent cause of his estrangement, exile, and death. It had often done so before, but the pang of this moment was as acute as if freshly given. She could hear the soft tone of his voice, as he said to her that day, "Can you trust me?" and she knew she *had* trusted him, had so relied on his generous nature, that she had felt sanguine of winning him home—of compelling him to give her a brother's love in return for that, which if not all he sought to win, would have been faithful, and pure, and true. And all had ended in this—that he slept unavenged in his far-off grave, and that she could do nothing to atone for the sorrow she had caused, but honour and mourn for his memory.

Was it the force of that memory, acting on her senses—or did she really hear a sound as if a key were once more turning in that lock? For a moment she was afraid her nerve was giving way, and that she had conjured up a vision out of her excited fancy; the next, she was recoiling in mortal fear, for the door was unlocked, and slowly, stealthily opening.

CHAPTER VIII.

GERVASE WRAY IS FAR FROM SATISFIED.

"If you please, sir," said Nancy, tapping at her master's door, "it is a note from Morlands, and to wait for an answer, please, sir."

Ungrammatical might be the information, but that was allowed to pass. The fact of a note from Morlands arriving before Mr. Brudenell was dressed, was important enough in itself, and full of alarming suggestions. The Vicar opened his door, and received it with a shaking hand. The last two years had aged him considerably, and his strength and nerve were by no means what they had been. He was a minute or two finding his glasses, and even then had a little difficulty in reading the note. Marion generally wrote a clear, bold hand, like her father; but this specimen looked very much as if it had been written in the dark, all the words jumbled up together. However, he deciphered it at last.

"As soon as you possibly can, dearest uncle, pray come to me. I want your advice on a matter of great importance, and every hour is of consequence. Tell no one but dear aunt. Come at once if you can.

"Your own M. C."

He read this three times over, and then called in his wife. "Read that, Maria."

She was quicker about it than he was, and looked at him in consternation. "What can be the matter? If any one was ill, she would have sent for me. What shall you do, Julian?"

"Send back the messenger, in the first place. Give me a pencil." He wrote on a slip of paper, "All shall be as you wish, my dear." And Mrs. Brudenell, whose toilet was by this time complete, went down herself to deliver it to the boy, with a cheerful word on the fineness of the morning. Neither he nor Nancy could have suspected any anxiety from her tone or manner. She lingered a few minutes, to make sure he was gone, then wrote a line to Cecil Percival, asking him to take the service that morning, despatched Nancy to his lodgings, and ordered a cup of coffee to be brought up for the Vicar without delay. It was only just put on the table when he came down.

"I have sent to Cecil, my dear, and as soon as you have swallowed this, you may go. Julian," almost in a whisper, "have you the remotest idea what she can want you for?"

"I can only conjecture that she may have had some painful news—perhaps about poor Saville. An application for money, perhaps —there is no knowing—and her husband being away, she sends for me. You will go with our friends to church as usual. If I want you, I will send a note. Be careful— the dear child evidently wishes not to excite curiosity."

"She has taken a queer way of carrying out her wishes. I declare, if it were any one but Marion, I should be very cross; but that child has sense, and it is that which alarms me."

It was rather difficult for Mrs. Brudenell to greet her guests, the Grahams, as they came down, one after another, and to behave herself as if nothing were on her mind but hospitable cares; but by hurrying them off to the early service, she escaped dangerous questions for the time. They supposed the Vicar to have gone on before, and when they found he was not in the church, could make no inquiries till afterwards. As they were returning, they saw him coming along the road. His tall form had begun to bend now, his hair was much whiter than it had been, and his walk was slow; but he was still the idol of the three Miss Grahams, who rushed to meet and escort him home.

"Why were you not at church, sir? Where have you been? You said you were going with us, and we should walk with you," were the clamorous greetings, to which he gently replied with a smile, that he could not be in two places at once, and that, like their papa, he was liable to be sent for at any moment.

"Were you sent for this morning? Was it for somebody who was very sick, and very poor, and very miserable indeed?" asked the youngest, shaking her head at each epithet.

"Yes, dear; and so I hope you will excuse my not keeping my appointment, and we will go in to breakfast."

The breakfast was a merry meal, and the little Grahams thought nothing had ever tasted so good; they were allowed to prattle to their hearts' content, and their parents listened smilingly, and thought how much good it must do their kind old friends to hear them. And when they could be heard themselves, they had questions to ask, and a great deal to say, about Morlands, and the Clarendons, and poor Harcourt's fate—topics on which people never grew tired of dilating—but which, just then, the Vicar would gladly have avoided. He had only given himself time to make a very slight repast, before he looked at his watch.

"I beg your pardon, Mrs. Graham, but I must ask you to excuse me. I have promised to pay another early visit this morning, and I see it is high time I set out. I shall not be detained long."

There was a general lament and remonstrance, but Mrs. Brudenell said nothing. She went on dispensing tea, and helping her guests to eggs, and ham, and hot rolls, and marmalade, with cheerful assiduity, until he was leaving the room; when she put down her teapot, and hastened after him. A few words—there was not time for more—passed between them; and then she came back to her place.

"I am afraid you do a little too much altogether," said Mrs. Graham, looking at her affectionately; "you are rather pale. Do not trouble yourself about us any more, but sit down, and have your own breakfast. Little people, if any one says another word before Mrs. Brudenell has had her cup of tea, I shall be really ashamed of you."

"No, no, let them chatter," said the hostess; "bless their hearts, they cannot be children all their lives—let them be happy while they may. Trouble comes soon enough, and heavy enough—sometimes where it is least looked for—but mercy comes with it, God be thanked, for all!"

Her voice suddenly failed; she put her handkerchief to her eyes, and hurried into the next room, where they heard her sobbing passionately.

The father and mother looked at each other, and at their astonished little ones; and whispered pitying words, of that sorrow which they believed their presence had revived in the childless mother's heart; and when Mrs. Brudenell came back, with red eyes, and an apology for being so foolish, she was received more lovingly than ever, without even the inquisitive youngest asking why she had cried.

Meanwhile, the Vicar had taken his way to the King's Arms, the Commercial Inn of

Stourbrooke—a place of some pretensions in the old coaching days, having a good name for ale and cheese. It stood very much on its respectability now, and the landlord was an ally of Mr. Brudenell's; and as the Vicar consulted his interest as far as possible, on all the festive occasions in which he took part, the host was always careful that nothing should be done contrary to Mr. Brudenell's wishes and opinion. With Mr. Percival, when he first came, he had a serious quarrel; but as his girls became the curate's ardent disciples, a truce was patched up by their intervention, and whenever they met now, it was on terms of the most guarded civility.

The sight of the Vicar walking into the bar at that early hour, surprised all who were there, and Mrs. Lloyd, the landlady, hurried out of her private parlour to make her curtsey, and ask if she could be of service. Mr. Brudenell explained he had come on a little matter of business with one of her guests—a French gentleman, M. Lepelletier.

"Gentleman, sir, do you call him?" quoth Mrs. Lloyd; "just like your kindness to everybody to give him such a name. He is here, sir—oh yes, he is here, and the sooner he goes the better I shall be pleased, for between ourselves, Mr. Brudenell," in a more cautious tone, "he gives me the impression of being one of the swell mob, and that's the truth. No gentleman would consort with such as he, *I* know."

The Vicar shook his head, but would not argue the point. "We will call him so till we find him behave otherwise, Mrs. Lloyd. Can I see him in a private room?"

"Certainly, Mr. Brudenell, sir, if you please. Will you send up your name?"

"No; merely that a gentleman wishes to see M. Lepelletier on business."

There was some delay before any notice was taken of this; and it transpired afterwards, that before trusting himself to the interview, M. Lepelletier took a private inspection of his visitor through the keyhole. That any danger could be hidden under that stooping form and those white locks, even his suspicious conscience could not anticipate, and he ventured at last to appear. Mr. Brudenell's first care was to ascertain that there were no listeners; he then went direct to the matter in hand.

"You called, sir, last evening, on Mrs. Clarendon of Morlands. It is from her that I am come to wait upon you. She has commissioned me to act for her, in the absence of Mr. Clarendon, so as to save you the trouble of calling again."

"She does me honour, M. le Curé."

"To tell you the truth, sir, I think she does you more honour than you are quite entitled to. I hesitate not to say, that you were not justified in applying to her personally at all."

"M. le Curé, permit me to differ from you. I have known Madame a long time; I know her past family troubles—I know a great deal —and I offer to Madame to buy my silence. If she will not, I have but to carry my goods to another market, you see."

"You spoke of a secret last night."

"I did, sir; a terrible secret. Will she buy it?"

"You named the terms. How are we to rely on your keeping your part of the contract?"

"My word of honour, sir, should be sufficient; or any oath you please."

"I shall profane no oaths by administering them to such as you, to whom honour is an empty name. Here is the money you asked for—money, won by George Saville, whom you tempted again and again to his ruin, and in winning which, he met the angel of God, telling him *that night his soul should be required of him.* His step-daughter has evidence that he repaid you, as you yourself well know; but she concedes that point, and sends you the full amount of your demand, on these conditions —that you breathe not a word to living being of what you know, and that you leave this place immediately."

He spread the bank-notes on the table; the Frenchman's eyes danced with greedy rapture.

"Ah, M. le Curé! you bring me new life. I will go this hour. And you would not hear my secret, though you pay for it?"

"No, sir; I wish to hear nothing. Do you accept the conditions?"

"Without reserve. You think me without honour; I will prove you are wrong. I swear to be silent—silent as the dead. Ah, M. le Curé! you believe everything; you believe the dead can rise and walk—yes? Then we are brothers in faith, for so do I. I take this money, and I kiss the fair hands of Madame. She has acted as a wise woman should, and she shall not repent. Ah! if George had but lived to see her now, in so fine a house, so rich, so well dressed! It was a pity to die so soon, and lose it all!"

"Oblige me, sir, by saying no more, but put up your money and make your arrangements to set off immediately. You have obtained your object, and your spoil. Take the advice of an old man, whom you may never see again, and lead a better life while you have time. It is not yet too late; you have been spared, when the man you tempted was cut off. That very money is a witness and a warning: let the evil it has done end here, and God forgive you what you have done yourself."

"Now do, Mr. Brudenell, sir," said Mrs. Lloyd, waylaying him as he passed out, "do have just a thimbleful of sherry before you walk home—you are looking so poorly this morning!"

"Not any, thank you. Your guest is going to leave you directly, Mrs. Lloyd. I shall be much obliged if you will let one of your lads follow him to the station, and bring me word when he has seen him off."

"It shall be done, sir; and a good riddance, say I, of all such rubbish as that. There is his bell ringing, to be sure, like the first lord in the land. Betsey!—24's bell!—If he asks for his bill, I am making it out this minute."

But 24 seemed in no hurry for his bill; his first care was to order a sumptuous breakfast, with hot meat, and the best wine in the cellar; and as this repast took some time in preparing, and was leisurely consumed, it was not till the middle of the day that he started for the station, in the fly belonging to the King's Arms—one of the stable-boys, by Mrs. Lloyd's orders, being mounted on the box.

The up-train was behind time, as usual, and while Lepelletier was sauntering along the platform, a down-train arrived, whence alighted two persons to whom his face was familiar. They stared at each other when they recognised him; and presently, Auguste stood before him, touching his hat, and requesting he would be good enough to step this way, where he would find his master.

"Ah, *mon cher M. Wray*, is it you? What happiness! I bless my good star that has detained me for this meeting."

"You have been doing business here?" asked Wray, significantly.

"A little—a very little. I have had the honour of calling on Madame Clarendon, and she has behaved quite like a lady. I have known her so long, I had no fear. Yes, yes, our little business is over."

"What business could you have with Mrs. Clarendon, I should like to know?"

"You would like—ah, yes!—but I am a man of honour—I never reveal a lady's secrets. She knows Achille Lepelletier, and that his heart is one stainless diamond. She appealed to it in the right way," slapping his pocket, "and it did not fail to respond. But *chut!* —not a word—this is all in confidence; and yonder comes my *convoi.* I wish you good morning."

Gervase Wray looked after him for a moment; then beckoned to his valet, to whom he gave some whispered instructions, seconded by a bank-note; and when the up-train started, it carried both Frenchmen with it to London. Wray watched them off, and stood so deep in thought as almost to have forgotten his own wants, till a porter, touching his hat, asked if he wanted a fly to Morlands, as there was one waiting from the King's Arms.

"To Morlands? Yes,—I do. Stay—drive me first to the White House;" and to the White House he was driven, musing the while on what he had just heard. What could Marion Clarendon have to conceal, that she should give money to that man? Some ugly business or other connected with George Saville, perhaps, which she was hushing up, lest it should come to the ears of her husband; nothing more likely. She was no friend of his, he was quite aware; and if this were true, she might have cause to regret it. He might find occasion to show her that it was worth her while to secure his good will; and he was deep in conjectures and probabilities, when he reached his destination.

Mrs. Porchester met him at the door.

"So glad you are come—I didn't breathe a syllable to Stella; it will be quite a surprise. I have been looking out for you the last hour, afraid to go up and dress for the déjeûner at Morlands, for fear you should come while I was up-stairs. Such a pity Roland could not come back in time; but your being here will be everything to me and Stella too."

"I wish I could believe that," said Gervase Wray. He had not time for more, as Stella came in at the moment, elegantly dressed for the festival, but wearing no festal aspect. She started at the sight of her visitor, and gave a sharp glance at her mother, which decided that good lady that it was high time she got ready too.

"I did nôt expect you to-day, Mr. Wray," said Stella, as soon as they were alone.

"I could not stay away any longer," was his reply, in a tone of some humility; "I have had long patience, but it fails me at times, and then I can hardly bear thē suspense."

"I thought I had ended your suspense," said she, coldly.

"It never can end while I have a hope left—and I must hope till you are married."

"I shall never marry. If you have only come to vex and torment me, I shall go up-stairs again, and send an excuse to Morlands. If you are in the humour to be pleasant and agreeable, you can follow me there with mamma. I promised Marion I would be early, to help her receive her guests."

"You are very intimate with Mrs. Clarendon, I suppose?"

"We meet often; I was there yesterday."

"Were you? Did she strike you as having anything on her mind, to cause her anxiety?"

"Only her husband's absence about that horrible affair—yes, by the way, I thought she did look a little worried by somebody who came on business in the evening, and insisted on her going to speak to him."

"Just so," said Gervase Wray, with a slight smile.

"What makes you ask? Do you know of anything?"

"No; I have my own opinion, that is all. Poor thing! The mischief some people do is not over when they are in their graves, and I should never be surprised to find her in some vexatious predicament, from her connexion with George Saville."

"You think this person had something to do with him?"

"I am nearly sure of it. I have just seen the man, and know who he is, and what he is—certainly, no one with whom she could have anything to do on her own account."

"It was very close of her to keep it from me," observed Stella.

"I think it was; you had a right to her confidence, as you put so much in her judgment, and act so entirely by her advice."

"Who told you that?"

"You tell it me yourself, by your coldness to me. I know she is not my advocate, and I need one sorely. Stella, dearest Stella, let me plead for myself." And as she did not forbid him in words, he seized his opportunity, and pleaded, so long and fluently, for a return of his affection, that Mrs. Porchester came down before an answer had been won. Her entrance gave Stella the means of evading it for the time, and she took care not to give him another chance before they all went to Morlands. He was satisfied with having obtained a hearing, and judiciously forbore to press her further.

The little Grahams were in the full delight of a game of croquet with some half-dozen small people, whose arrival had already inaugurated the fête. Mrs. Lyndsay was amusing herself by assisting them, and informed the new comers that Miss Clarendon had been a little fractious that morning, and absorbed her mamma entirely. A council of matrons was already sitting on the case, but of course Mrs. Porchester would be admitted. Before Mrs. Porchester could make her way up-stairs, Marion came down. She, too, was surprised to see Gervase; and his easy apologies, calling for hospitable welcome as a matter of course, irritated her beyond power of concealment. He saw it plainly enough, but he had made up his mind to remain, and she had no choice, but to beg he would occupy his old quarters as usual.

Stella took the first opportunity of drawing her aside. "It was not my doing, Marion. I suspect he knows everything I do, or you either; and when we would not invite him, resolved to come uninvited. I have long thought Jones was a spy, and now I know it."

"Why then do you not send her away?"

"Because, my dear, we should have to pay her wages. Why do I not send him away too, but because I do not know how soon I may be driven to accept him? You would not suppose, to look at me, what letters I have had to write this morning. Marion, you promised me help, but you never gave it."

"Roland has been away," murmured Marion, with downcast eyes.

"When do you expect him back?"

"He may appear any day. I heard from him this morning, and he says, by the time I receive his letter, he would be on his way home; so I cannot write to him."

"And you cannot help me, Marion? I am ashamed to ask you, but two or three hundred pounds just now would be of more value than thousands at another time. I could pay the most urgent cases something on account, and then I should have some peace. And what would a sum like that be to Roland?"

"If I had it to give you—if I had any right," faltered Marion, whose agitation had increased with every word, "I would not hesitate; but you must believe me—I can do nothing till Roland comes home—and I dare not promise it, even then."

"You have promised already," said Stella, reproachfully.

"I have promised to do what I could—that I promise still, but no more. Do not ask me again."

"I certainly will not. It is the first time I ever did ask such a favour, and if I had not felt I was speaking to a sister and friend, I should not have asked it at all. Pray think no more about it; it is of no consequence. What is that tiresome dog fidgeting about?"

For Nelson had come into the morning-room, and after snuffing in every direction with an uneasy air, began pawing his mistress, as if to attract her attention.

"He wants to be let out for a run. Come, Nelson!" said Mrs. Clarendon, hastily opening the window, "out, good dog, fetch!"

But neither "out" nor "fetch," answered the good dog's purpose; he declined going into the garden, and continued to fawn on Marion. "He wants water, perhaps," said she, moving to the door; and directly she did so, he began to bound with joy. In the doorway stood Gervase Wray.

"I found Nelson lying before the private door," he said, in a low voice, "and when I patted him he came off to look for you. How tenacious a dog's memory is! Let us see where he wants you to go."

Marion shrank back. Nelson took hold of her dress, and tried to pull her on.

"You must go with him," said Stella, "if only out of curiosity;" and they both accompanied her, as she reluctantly followed Nelson to his former post at the door of the secluded apartments. Here he stopped, and began scratching vigorously.

"He wants to go in," observed Gervase, quietly.

"He ought to know better," said Marion. "Nelson! Down directly, sir!"

Nelson ceased scratching, but snuffed under the door, and sat down with his ears put back, and his eyes full of expectation.

"He smells rats, perhaps," suggested Stella. "Why not go in and see if there is anything?"

Marion made no reply, but walking on, called Richards to take Nelson and shut him up—a mandate that was not very easy to obey, as his reluctance was extreme; but his mistress was inexorable. The sounds of carriage-wheels driving up compelled her to repair to the drawing-room, and Gervase and Stella walked into the garden. "What do you think?" he asked, when they were safely out of hearing; "is she not rather odd and excited to-day?"

"I think she is."

"Do you know, I am afraid she has been imposed upon; she is very generous, and I know Roland allows her to draw for what she pleases. That person I told you of, for instance, he could not have much claim on her, and I know she was very liberal to him, for he boasted of it."

He stole a glance at Stella's burning face, and saw the shaft had told. "She could give to a man like that, and pretend to me that she could do nothing in Roland's absence!" thought Miss Porchester, and she bit her lip, and began to talk gaily on other matters. Mr. Wray followed her lead, and in the rapid arrival of guests, Stella's attention was soon devoted, perforce; but her companion being less in request, watched his opportunity, and went round to the stables. He was so well known as the friend of the family, that all the servants were ready to do his bidding, and no difficulty was made about the release of Nelson. The dog, who had been howling ever since his incarceration, jumped upon him in delight at regaining his liberty; and after snuffing about a few minutes, trotted off into the house. Gervase followed, and found him watching as before.

"Now, what can this mean?" thought he, as he stood observing the dog's movements. "Good old fellow—seek! fetch him out!"

Nelson began to scratch the door, and finding it to no purpose, gave an impatient howl. His mistress heard it from the drawing-room, and came in a moment. "Nelson! come away, sir! Who let him loose without my leave?"

"It was my fault, Mrs. Clarendon; the poor dog yelled so piteously, I thought I would give him a run, but he slipped away, and came back here. I should really be inclined to think you must have rats on this floor."

"I cannot have him disturbing the house in this way," said Marion; "come here, Nelson, come!" The dog obeyed reluctantly. She led the way to a little room, where Roland stowed away whips, fishing-tackle, and great-coats, and taking one of the latter, laid it on the floor. "Watch, Nelson!" The dog smelt the coat, walked round it inquisitively, and finally lay down upon it, with his ears back, and his eyes on his mistress.

"He will not stir now till I bid him," said she; "I would advise no one to try and take that coat away."

"Nelson owns your power, as we all do," said Gervase Wray, smiling; "I only wish it were sometimes exercised for me."

"In what way?"

"In the way that would ensure my happiness. You have great influence over Miss Porchester—if I could only think you were my friend!"

"My husband's friend must be mine, Mr. Wray, but if Miss Porchester does not love you, what good would my influence do?"

"I believe I should have a chance, if I had some one at hand to plead for me; and, Mrs. Clarendon, no one can be that friend but yourself."

Marion shook her head. "You must not ask me; it is not in my power."

"You are only a friend in name, then?"

"In deed also, I hope, should you really want me. It would be no friendship to persuade my cousin to marry you unless she loved you first."

"I would take my chance of that—I would win her afterwards—will you try?"

"On no account whatever. I am sorry to be obliged to say this; if you have any regard for me, you will not ask it again. I hope you will find everything comfortable in your room—they tell me you have not brought your servant."

"No; he came with me as far as the station, and there he met a *compatriote*, and I gave him leave to go back with him."

"You are indeed an indulgent master."

"I believe I am; there might be a little self-interest in my indulgence, for I had reason to suspect the other fellow was in possession of information I wished to acquire, and Auguste will do his best to get it out of him."

"Was the person any one I know?" asked Marion, steadily.

"I believe you may remember the name—Lepelletier."

"Yes, I do indeed. What made you suspect he knew anything worth knowing?"

"I had my reasons. At any rate, there is no harm done by making sure. Auguste is like a bloodhound on the trail of a secret, and he will not show his face to me till he has followed it up."

"Did he tell you that he had seen me?"

Wray had not expected this question. "Yes," he replied, with a slight change of colour.

"I thought so, by your manner; you were waiting to see if that were a secret too. He came last night to ask me for money, which he said Mr. Saville had borrowed. My uncle settled with him this morning, and sent him away."

"Indeed! I wonder you gave him anything in Clarendon's absence."

"I believe I am the best judge of that. Perhaps, if you let Auguste know what I have told you, it will satisfy his curiosity without further trouble."

"I beg your pardon, Mrs. Clarendon; but with a man like that you may be sure there is always something that does not at first appear. One of his objects may have been to extort your money—what else he had in view we shall learn by-and-by. It is rather a rash thing to begin paying such demands without investigation."

"I know it is, but I have done it, and I wish you would tell Auguste to let him alone. No good can come of any intercourse with him, and he is as likely as not to rob the poor fellow, if he persuades him to play."

"If I had known you had been paying him on demand, I should certainly have kept them apart, for Auguste, in strict confidence, has a similar grievance on his mind, and he will think it hard that one should be removed and not another."

"What is his claim?" asked Marion, with a sigh. The look of patient suffering in her face would at any other time have moved his compassionate interest—now it only made him more suspicious.

"I do not quite know the amount, but I believe it is rather more than a thousand francs—forty pounds—a trifle to us, but being all his savings, a great loss to him."

"Write to him, Mr. Wray, by this post,

will you, and tell him you have named it to me, and that I will let him have the money, on condition of his having nothing to do with M. Lepelletier. He will not venture to deceive you on that point, I suppose, and I think you will agree with me that no good can arise from their being together."

"You make this a condition, then?"

"Certainly; I have paid M. Lepelletier quite enough—I have no wish to tempt him to plunder a poor servant."

"I honour your generosity and frankness; I will write at once."

He turned into the library, wrote his note, and then strolled into the grounds to find Stella. She was waiting for her turn at croquet, and seemed unwilling to be drawn aside.

"Did I not tell you how generous Mrs. Clarendon can be? Read that."

Stella read, and gave it back impatiently.

"Did you really ask her to do it?"

"I only told her, as she had paid one claimant, the other would feel ill used, and that was her reply. You look as if it disgusted you."

"I feel disgusted with everybody—you are all alike, and I can understand none of you."

"Do you not understand what this means?

It is to stop Auguste's investigations. There is some mystery going on; what it is, I cannot pretend to say, but I am convinced of one thing," he lowered his voice, and looked cautiously round, "whatever it may be, it is connected with Harcourt's rooms."

CHAPTER IX.

HOW ROLAND FOUND WHAT HE SOUGHT.

The day wore on, and the fête was in full progress. Everybody pronounced it a complete success, so far; and all were doing their best, as the evening advanced, to carry it successfully to an end. Long had it been since the ball-room had echoed with the sound of gay feet and spirited music; and though it was longer than the numbers of the party required, no one found fault with having too much space. It was not a ball, and therefore nobody expected to be crushed, and the children danced with the elders, and stoutly repudiating the notion of fatigue, decided that Morlands was some ten degrees better than fairyland. The little Grahams had never spent such a day of bliss: they had seen all the horses, all the fancy poultry, the dairy, and the gardens; they had played croquet, and rowed in the boat, and had beautiful things to eat, at the long table, as if they had been grown up; and now they were staying up "ever so late," to dance with tall gentlemen, with the alluring prospect of supper by-and-by. They wished there could be a christening fête at Morlands once a week—their only drawback had been the seclusion of the baby. That poor little innocent, in whose honour they were enjoying themselves, had been far too fretful all day to be brought among the guests; and anxiety on her account added, in no small degree, to the burden that sat too heavily on the young mother to be entirely concealed. Mrs. Brudenell did her best for her, by devoting herself to the child up-stairs, and Stella and Mrs. Lyndsay were equally zealous below; but not the less did she feel as if the day would never be over, and that to be rid of all her joyous visitors would be a relief beyond price. She was kneeling by her aunt, across whose lap the little one was lying, and they were agreeing that it would be a satisfaction to see Dr. Wartop, when Mrs. Peters put her head in, and whispered a request to speak to her mistress.

"Come in, Peters; we are alone," said Marion.

"I beg your pardon, ma'am—if I could speak to you here——"

Marion looked at her aunt, and hurried to obey the summons. The colloquy was not long, but it had driven all the colour from her cheeks when she returned.

"I have sent for him," she whispered. Mrs. Brudenell turned pale herself.

"Is it necessary——?" Marion bowed her head, and looked wistfully at the baby.

"I must go," she said, slowly, "and if it be what she thinks, and what I fear—you will help me to see my duty. Can I have done her harm already?"

"I trust not, darling; do not frighten yourself. The calmer you are, the better it will be for you both. Perhaps it would be more prudent not to take her till you are sure. I will not leave her a moment, so go down, and show yourself. You can explain to some of them that the pet is not well, and they will think nothing of your sending for the Doctor."

"Oh, here is our hostess at last!" said Mrs. Lyndsay, as Marion appeared in the ball-room. "I do think we are very cruel to go on amusing ourselves when you are so anxious. How is the dear child now?"

"Not well; I have sent for our Doctor—my aunt thinks it quite right to do so."

"And you, poor thing, wish us all anywhere out of the way, for keeping you from your darling. But I hope she will be all right to-morrow. Mrs. Porchester says it is nothing to make you uneasy. How charmingly everything has gone off! Stella has excelled herself, and it is easy to see who is her slave. Do you think I might meddle in that matter as I did in another, and advise imprudence as the best wisdom?"

Marion smiled, but not in assent.

"To marry on love only may be imprudent—but to marry on money only——"

"Might be madness, you think. Perhaps I had better let well alone. I am quite content with my one success. You were very ungrateful, though, for we never had a secretary to our mind, and my father always declares Roland was just what he wanted. I wish you were obliged to retrench, and required a small addition to your income."

"Tell me, Florence," said Marion, in a low, hurried tone, "if my husband should feel he wanted work and wished for an appointment, could he really get one?"

"Get one? No doubt he could, but such

an appointment as he would care to accept is not vacant every day."

"I mean something like the secretaryship —supposing he wished for such occupation."

"My dear, if he were but crazy enough to wish for that, we should dance for joy. I want to see my father made comfortable with a real gentleman about him, and such a good fellow as Roland would be too great luck to hope for. I can safely promise you the refusal of it, I dare say, if your husband's time as a country gentleman hangs heavy on his hands."

"Mrs. Clarendon," whispered a voice in her ear, "did you see Nelson just now?"

"No; I thought he was in the stable. I sent him there to have his supper."

"He has forced his way out, then, and is again at that door. I wonder you can think of going to bed to-night with such a mystery unsolved."

"If you are nervous about it, Mr. Wray, I dare say Mrs. Porchester would give you a bed at the White House. Shall I ask her?"

He made no reply, and took the first opportunity of passing on.

"You were quite right to put him down," said Mrs. Lyndsay; "he is too inquisitive by half. I hate men to be always prying into everything one does, and his curiosity is an insatiable gulf. But tell me, dear, are those really the rooms where poor Harcourt used to shut himself up? My father thought they were, but was not sure."

"They are," said Marion.

"Might we see them, do you think? I should like it so much. I was very fond of the poor fellow when we were children—he was not a man generally understood, or appreciated."

"I cannot show the rooms to any one in Roland's absence."

"Really? Not even to me?"

"Not even to you, my dear Florence, kind as you have always been to me. No one ever goes into them but myself and my housekeeper."

"Do you think I should be less discreet, or less reverent, in my poor cousin's rooms, than good Mrs. Peters?"

"No; but you are a stranger there, and she is not."

"Well, I will not be intrusive. Does Stella know those rooms?"

"She may have seen them formerly—never since——"

"Ah, very well, I will not ask you again. I am sorry I have teased so much already."

And meeting Stella soon afterwards, she told her the purport of their conversation, which Stella, in turn, repeated in the course of the evening to Mr. Wray.

A little while after supper, a rumour circulated among the guests, that the Doctor was in the house, and very uneasy about the dear little baby. The music ceased, the dancers stood about in whispering dismay, and every one asked questions of those who were supposed to have special means of information, without anybody being able to give satisfactory answers. The hostess had disappeared entirely, and those who had ventured on expeditions of inquiry had not been allowed to disturb the conference in Mrs. Clarendon's room, where the child now was. At last, to the general relief, Mrs. Brudènell appeared, and as soon as she could make herself heard in the clamour that surrounded her, explained that Dr. Wartop could not exactly pronounce on the baby's attack yet—but he was going to remain for the night, and, as the quieter the house was kept the better, it would be as well that the party should break up at once. Mrs. Graham would go back to the Vicarage with her young folks, and take the management of the house, as she herself must remain with Marion.

Regrets and alarm were universal, and old Mr. Percival eagerly drew her aside to ask if it would not be better for Mrs. Clarendon to have no guests on her mind, and might he be permitted to invite them to the Hall? On her owning that it would be the best plan, he proceeded to urge it on the General and Mrs. Lyndsay, and such of the visitors as were to sleep at Morlands; and though there was some demur at first, at leaving Marion in such trouble, it was finally decided that it might be greater kindness than remaining. No time was lost in making the needful arrangements. All agreed, with the exception of Gervase Wray, who resisted persuasion and argument, simply maintaining that in Roland's absence he might possibly be useful; and therefore, unless turned out as an incumbrance, he should prefer to stay. And as no one could do that, he did stay, and saw the last lights of the deserted banquet-hall put out by Richards, and yet lingered about the room, as if the scent of fading flowers and extinguished wax-candles had a more soothing charm than is usually attributed thereto. Here Mr. Brudenell found him, after seeing his friends home.

"This is dull work for you, Mr. Wray. Do not stay here in the dark; there are lights in the library, and I shall be glad to join you there, as we must give Dr. Wartop some supper presently."

"I have no wish for any supper, thank you, sir."

"But the Doctor has, and I must ask you to act as host in Roland's absence. I would stay to-night if I could, but I cannot leave my own guests quite deserted."

He had drawn Wray on while speaking, and they were soon in the library, where the butler was placing a tray of refreshments.

"It is a pity you should stay from your friends," said Gervase. "You look very tired as it is. Trust to me—I will take care of the Doctor."

"Thank you; then I will just speak to my wife, and send him down to you."

As soon as the Vicar had left him, Mr. Wray rang the bell. "Richards, where is Nelson?"

"In the stable, sir."

"I hate his being there, poor fellow. Just have him put in my room, will you? I am never quite comfortable without a dog near me."

Richards bowed; he had long been used to take Mr. Wray's orders, and never thought of disputing them. By-and-by came Dr. Wartop, but in no caustic, fault-finding humour. He was silent, grave, almost gentle, and very thirsty. Gervase Wray was alarmed by these symptoms, and after vainly endeavouring to rouse his companion to something like his usual frank vivacity of speech, asked if he had any fears about the infant?

"Yes," quoth the Doctor.

"Is it then so bad a case already?" asked Wray, really shocked.

"I do not know what you mean by 'so bad,' but we want the father home. How is one to get at him?"

"He is on his way home, we believe."

"Do you know what route he will take?"

"No; Mrs. Clarendon will probably hear to-morrow."

"Ah! Well, sir, I recommend you now to go to bed, and let the poor servants do the same. There will be nothing for any of you to do to-night."

"Doctor, how is Mrs. Clarendon herself?"

"Why do you ask, when you have been with her all day?"

"Just for that reason; she seemed to me not quite herself. Her friends went away really uneasy about her."

"They were quite right," said Dr. Wartop, gravely; "and I shall keep her quiet to-morrow. If people will give parties, and stand about all day, when they have young children to nurse," added he, with a sudden burst of his old spleen, "it is not to be wondered at if they are ill, and keep one up all night to see after them. Do not let us keep *you* up, though, Mr. Wray, as we may want to make you useful to-morrow. I shall be glad to have the house quiet. The shutting of doors and tramping along galleries are the very worst things that a patient can fight against."

So Gervase Wray was fain to go to his room, and, with Nelson for company, sat patiently waiting till the house was perfectly still. About two o'clock he opened his door, and listened; not a sound could he hear but Nelson's tail lazily beating the floor, as he watched him from his curled-up attitude of rest. Wray left his room, and glanced over the balusters of the wide staircase—as he did, he saw the glimmer of a moving light below. It was but momentary—then all was dark as before. He stepped back to his room for a candle, whistled softly to the dog, who took some rousing before he would move, and went down with him to the door which Nelson had watched in the day. "Seek, good dog," he whispered, patting him on the back.

Nelson sought—smelt—listened—and took him by surprise with a fierce and angry fit of barking, quite beyond Wray's power to silence. The door opened suddenly, and Marion stood before him. Pale, almost ghastly, as her face was when the light fell upon it, it flushed in a moment as she recognised her visitor.

"What does this mean? What are you doing here, Mr. Wray? Why do you bring the dog here again?"

He began an incoherent apology, to which she gave no heed.

"Take him away—take him away," she said, as Nelson fawned upon her for admittance, "and go back to your room. I could not have believed this of you; but excuses only make it worse. Go, sir, this moment!"

She had closed the door behind her, and stood waiting for him to obey.

"You mistake me, Mrs. Clarendon," he said, with some humility; "I could not sleep for anxiety, and—and I thought I heard some one breaking into the house—and so——"

"And so you fetched the dog to bark at this door, which you knew to be locked. I am sorry you have been disturbed, Mr. Wray; now you are satisfied that there are no thieves in the house, perhaps you will sleep better."

"I beg your pardon, Mrs. Clarendon—I am far from satisfied—I am more alarmed than I was before." He paused, and held the light so as to read her countenance more distinctly. He had already noted that she was in a plain morning dress, instead of the one she had worn in the evening. "I am more alarmed than if I had found a thief in the house, for what he took you might replace; but if it were possible that, from a false generosity, an overstrained mercy, you had been induced to risk your husband's anger to save a miscreant——"

"Be silent, sir!" she said, with flashing eyes. "No one shall presume to speak so to me in my own house! Oh no, Mr. Wray, I did not mean to be so hasty—I have no right to be so imperious—but you try me beyond my patience, and I cannot bear much more."

"My respect forbids me to reply," he said, with a bow, as he retired, leaving her standing before the door, where she remained till he was out of sight.

He was bitterly chagrined by this incident; it placed him in an awkward position in a house where he had always been careful to maintain an easy one; and he was quite aware that if the story were told, his vague suspicions would not appear a satisfactory reason for playing the spy on his hostess in the middle of the night. The more he thought it over, the more convinced he was that something secret was going on, and that his conjecture was the true one; but he had so completely put himself in the wrong, that he did not like the prospect of facing Marion in the morning, and began to feel something towards her very like hatred. He was not a malevolent man, but he was small-souled, and had been long accustomed to do little mean things, of which he was not ashamed, because they were cleverly disguised, and that small soul felt now sorely aggrieved, and longed for a fair opening for retaliation. Morning broke while he was considering what to do, and with the light came a visitor to his room—it was Dr. Wartop.

"I have just come to tell you, Mr. Wray, how sorry I am you were disturbed last night. I found I had forgotten some medicine I meant to bring with me, and I thought I might find some in poor Clarendon's den. He was fond of dabbling in medicine, as well as in other things. I had no idea we were so noisy as to rouse you and Nelson. You startled Mrs. Clarendon, by the way, and she has not yet got over it."

"I am very sorry; pray make her my best apologies. What of the child?"

"The child is better; I am more anxious about the mother. She will keep her room to-day, and I should strongly advise you not to stay. It only makes her anxious and nervous to have any one in the house to think about."

"I quite understand, Doctor, and I shall start as soon as the letters have come in. I heartily wish Clarendon were come home."

He rang the bell, requested some breakfast immediately, and a carriage to take him to the station, as soon as the post-bag had been delivered, which always appeared at eight. As he expected, among a packet of letters forwarded from his lodgings, was one from Roland, telling him he might be in London any day, and should put up at his old quarters, until he had had an interview with the authorities of the detective police: he had reason to believe the assassin had returned to England, and if so, he would find him, alive or dead. Wray read this over two or three times, then called the servant to take down his portmanteau, and left Morlands without again seeing any of its inmates.

He reached his lodgings early in the day; found that his servant was out, and nothing had been seen of Mr. Clarendon. He was in time still, at any rate, and he wrote his letters, and waited impatiently for the appearance of his valet. Still, no valet came, and he made more inquiries. Auguste had arrived the evening before, and announced his intention of sleeping there, but went out again soon after, and did not return till five in the morning—stayed an hour, and went away again, in a cab, taking some boxes with him.

"Had he heard from me?" asked Wray of his informant.

"No, sir, I think not; at least, there is a letter below that came for him after he had left. He was gone before post time, and we have seen nothing of him since."

A misgiving seized Gervase Wray; he went into his bedroom, looked into his drawers, and then ran back to examine his writing-table. All had been ransacked, and everything of value was gone.

It was late in the afternoon of the following day—a day that had been oppressively hot, very like the one on which Marion had first come to Stourbrooke—when Widow Trail awoke from a short doze into which she had fallen after hours of suffering; and turning her eyes towards the light, perceived Cecil Percival standing at a little distance.

"Won't she come?" was the question her lips tried to frame, but they were so dry and parched, the words were hardly to be heard. He knew her meaning, and having gently moistened her mouth, smiled as he said, "I told you she would, and here she is. She has left her sick child to come to you, because you ask it, so we must not keep her long."

"I'll not keep her long—I'll trouble none o' you long—but I wanted to see her again—yes, I did." And as Marion came slowly forward, and stood by the bed, the old woman's eyes rested upon her with a pleading in their gaze that gave her dull features a transient dignity.

"I'm going fast, my deary, I am—I shan't trouble anybody much longer."

"You are in less pain, I hope?" said Marion. There was a convulsive aching in her throat that would hardly allow her to speak.

"I'm very bad, that's what I am, and I can't die—no, I can't till you ease my mind, deary. I know it's hard what I'm going to ask, but will you, will you now——" She got hold of the young lady's wrist, and clutched it with her yellow, bony fingers—"will you try and not think too badly of my poor Bob? I know he wur a wild one—he allus wur—and minded nobody—but if you'd heard how he talked of the Squire, you'd never believe he'd go for to do him a mischief, never. He couldn't abide your master, that he couldn't—but Mr. Clarendon—I don't think he'd ha' touched a hair of his head—leastways, if he did, it wurn't Bob himself, it wur the drink, that's what it wur; and when the drink gets into a man—oh deary, deary me! haven't I seen enough o' what comes o' that? It's a hard world, a very hard world, for poor old bodies. I'm glad to get out of it, and they'll all be glad to be rid o' me."

"You are going to a better, I hope."

"'Deed, and I hope so too, my deary, or it won't be worth while to go at all. And if you'd only ease my mind, as I wur saying, I'd just like a bit of prayer, and not trouble none o' you any more. You will try, won't you, deary?"

The large tears that had been gathering in Marion's eyes dropped heavily on her cheeks, as she knelt down by the bed.

"Will you," she said, "forgive us in return, if we have been unjust to him?"

Percival came a step nearer, and bent down to hear the answer. It came out with almost a snarl. "No, I won't! If you've been unjust to my poor lad, it will be visited upon you—ay, it will! There's One who cares for the poor, and He'll see him righted, though I shan't. There's Mr. Percival will tell you that—ask him!"

Marion looked up at Cecil with eyes that seemed imploring his mercy. Their glances met, and before the grave, alarmed questioning of his, her head drooped sadly, and she covered her face with her hands. The old woman was touched by her distress.

"Lawks, my poor lovey, I didn't mean to say nothin' against you, nor yet your master. They say he's a hasty young gentleman, but I dare say he's a kind one; they're mostly kind when they has what they wants, and keeps away from the drink. Oh, I'm thirsty—give me some'at." Marion gave her some spoonfuls of lemonade. "That's good, thank ye kindly. The Lord will pay it back to you; and you'll try and think kindly of poor Bob, won't you?"

"I promise you faithfully," said Marion.

"Then now I'm easy, and if he'll read me a bit o' prayer, I'll go to sleep."

Again Marion looked at Mr. Percival, expecting him to begin at once, but he remained silent and motionless. The old woman expressed no surprise; she was gradually becoming torpid; but the silence perplexed Mrs. Clarendon, and she whispered nervously, "Will you not do as she asks?"

"God help me!" was all his answer, and he burst into an agony of such tears as she had never seen before.

"God help us all," she repeated, "for we all need help sorely; but she is going fast, and it will soon be too late. Who can comfort her if you cannot?"

"What right have I to give comfort, or speak peace? How can I do the priest's office with a lie in my right hand? Can you answer me that? No, how should you, innocent and true as you are? Go, you have done your part; your uncle will soon be here, and to his faithful hands the work shall be left, for which mine are utterly unworthy."

Even as he spoke, the Vicar's slow step was on the stairs, and as he entered the sick-chamber, his lips pronounced the blessing for which all three were thirsting in vain.

The short service was over, and Marion was moving to the door.

"If you will wait for me below, my love," said her uncle, "I will see you home. I have a word to say to Percival first."

She went below, and would have waited, feeling exhausted in body and mind, but Mrs. Andrews, who was an old ally of Mrs. Brudenell's, had been on the watch, and came out directly she appeared.

"Oh, Mrs. Clarendon, ma'am, if you please, Mr. Clarendon was here just a minute or two ago, and he asked how Mr. Percival was, and I told him you was both with the poor sick body up-stairs, and you'll excuse my telling you, ma'am, though it do seem a liberty, but he was not quite pleased, and he has driven on home, and I thought you'd rather know directly, you see, ma'am. I beg your pardon, and his, I'm sure, for being so bold."

She had said quite enough; Marion almost flew out of the house, and along her way home; the distance seeming threefold its usual length, and her limbs as if made of lead. The fly was not out of sight; Roland was stopping it now to speak to Stella and Mrs. Lyndsay; what would they be telling him? Oh, if she could only make him stop! He was getting out to walk with them—would he not even look round to see if she was coming? Yes, he had turned, he saw her, they were waiting; and now he came striding back to meet her, and his face was flushed and dark, and his lips tightly compressed. He said not a word, but offered his arm, which she took and clung to, panting and nearly spent. Happen what might, condemn her unheard as he seemed disposed to do, there was relief and comfort in his presence that his anger could not quite take away. Not a word was spoken, as they walked on to join their relations, who were watching the meeting with no small curiosity.

"It is a real comfort to see you out, Marion," said Mrs. Lyndsay, "for it is a proof baby is better. I do believe you only wanted to get rid of us, and primed the Doctor to give the alarm. Now we may be admitted again, I hope, and judge for ourselves."

"Not to-day," said Marion, faintly; "she is not yet well enough to be disturbed; we are not sure yet what it will prove to be."

"Yet you left her to go *there*," murmured Roland, in a tone that no one heard but herself, and was rather hard to bear.

"It was time Roland came back," observed Stella, "for Morlands has been lately like a Castle of Udolpho. Gervase Wray, like a *preux chevalier*, tried sleeping in it, but was nearly throttled in the night by old Nelson, and fled at cock-crow, leaving no trace behind. Do you bring any news of the recreant, Roland?"

"Yes; that Auguste has robbed him, not only of money and plate, but of private papers and letters, which Wray thinks the greater loss of the two—for some of them were yours."

"So?" said Mrs. Lyndsay, archly, glancing at Miss Porchester, whose face had darkened visibly; "no wonder the poor man is in despair. Well, we must hope he will catch the thief; and now we will leave you two to talk about the baby in peace, which you are longing to do. I am going to dine at the White House, as Mr. Percival has taken my father to a club dinner at some old inn, famous for its port wine. It will be a miracle if he escapes the gout. By the way, Marion, my dear, there is an appointment vacant now, if you will have it. You can let me know to-morrow. Only be in time, r these good things are snapped up in a moment."

In this style they talked, Marion alone remaining silent, till they reached the gate into the grounds; here the two ladies left them, to walk across the park, and the Clarendons hurried on to the house. It was all Marion could do, and yet even Roland was not more impatient for its shelter than she was. He asked no questions till he had brought her into the library, and given her a glass of wine and water; but he stood by her as she drank it, with a severity in his face that showed how keenly he felt.

"Can you answer me now, Marion?" he said, when he saw she was a little recovered.

"Roland, dearest, do not be angry with me —I could not help it—I have a great deal to tell you, if you will only give me time and courage."

"Courage, Marion? what have you to fear with me?" He saw she was faint with agitation, but it only served to excite him the more. "Do you think I care for what Gervase chose to say? Do you think I would stand and hear it said that you had mysteries and secrets which you were afraid of his finding out—actually implying, that out of goodness of heart, you might have been induced to have anything to do with that execrable——"

"Hush, hush, my dearest—God forgive you the word! He will, for you know not what you do."

And she threw herself on his breast, and sobbed hysterically, unable, at first, to control her emotion, although she knew every moment's delay added to the fever of irritated impatience, which all his tenderness could not quite overcome. The more she sobbed and trembled, the darker his suspicions became.

"Marion," he said, sternly, "there is only one thing possible for you to have done, which it would be impossible for me to forgive.

When Wray hinted at it, I nearly knocked him down—we shall never be again the friends we were—and if I thought such things had been done in this house—in those rooms—sacred to that dear memory which I have sworn to see avenged——"

"Stop, Roland, stop—I must not hear that word—it is not for us. Come with me, and I will show you why."

Her paleness had given place to a sudden glow of excitement, and her husband was startled by the strange expression of her eyes, in which pity, terror, grief, and gladness, seemed striving for the mastery by turns. It silenced the question on his lips, and obeying her gesture of caution, he followed in increasing wonder and dread—dread that became almost insupportable when she opened the private door, and secured it behind them as soon as they had entered. "Marion! why have you dared to bring me here?"

"To tell you what I was afraid of any one overhearing. Roland, a great mercy has been granted to us, but it brings with it difficulty and danger. Have you strength and courage to command yourself—not for your own sake only?"

She had hoped that by guessing at her meaning he might escape the shock her experience had taught her to dread; but as if stung to sudden madness by confirmed suspicion, he seized her hands in his strong grasp, so passionately as to give her acute pain for some time afterwards. "I will never forgive you, Marion!" sounded like thunder in her ears, as he thrust her off, before she could speak again, and rushed past her into the workroom, where sat Dr. Wartop, mixing some powders.

"You here, too? Why are you not with the child? Who are you attending here without my leave, sir?"

"Hush, sir, if you please; it is *my* leave you will have to ask, before you go any farther. Mrs. Clarendon, does he know——?"

"Dearest Roland, only hear me one moment——" pleaded Marion, but she was cut short.

"I insist on seeing who is here—who is desecrating these rooms—who has dared—— Oh, merciful Heaven! what is that?"

For a voice from the inner room was calling, "Roland!" and it was the voice of Harcourt, his brother.

CHAPTER X.

REUNITED.

The first stunning shock of such a joy is almost as hard to bear as that of grief; and Roland, though he did not lose his senses, never knew exactly what happened, till, by degrees, as full consciousness returned, he realised that he was kneeling by his brother's bed, and that their arms were locked round each other. What words passed between them in that first moment of reunion, their angels may have heard, but no one else; even Marion drew reverently back, not to disturb such a foretaste of the promised bliss; and though watching both so as to be ready with assistance the instant it was needed, did her best to help them to forget her. And at first she was forgotten; there was no room in Roland's heart for any thought but of the risen from the dead. He could not recall that they had parted in anger, when they met in such a clasp of love; and it was not till Harcourt murmured the word "forgiveness," that he remembered he had both to ask and to receive.

"Noll, dear old Noll—how could I ever think you unkind? I know I often provoked you, but if you knew how I have grieved since I thought you dead—how every little thing I ever did to vex you, has made my heart ache, you would forgive me. Do you remember my driving Stella against your orders? I have often wished I had cut my hand off first. Where have you been? How is it you escaped? And why are you hidden here, instead of being welcomed in your own house? What has Marion been thinking of?"

"Of what has not yet struck you, dear fellow," said Harcourt. His voice was weak, but mournfully earnest; and as his brother raised himself to look at him, he fixed his sunken eyes on his face, with a strange mixture of shame and pity. Roland gazed at him in wonder at first, but gradually, as he began to understand, the dazzling joy faded from his countenance, and a horror of great darkness came down upon his soul. Marion saw it coming; she had been waiting for that moment, and was directly by his side, with her arm on his shoulder.

"Roland, he is in danger—we must think of that only—we must command ourselves—no one must suspect he is here. No one knows it but Dr. Wartop, my uncle and aunt, and Peters, and they will stand by us through everything. He wants all our help, and all our love; and on whose should he rely, if not on yours and mine?"

Roland, who had crouched down by the bed, and buried his face between his arms, now lifted it up.

"Tell me the worst at once—what became of Trail?"

There was an expressive silence—his head sank lower than before.

"God is my witness," said Harcourt—no words can describe the sadness with which he spoke—"I had no intention to hurt him. We had walked a long way, and he had been drinking without my knowledge, and when I spoke sharply to him for his behaviour, he suddenly pulled out one of my pistols. I thought he must be going mad, and hit out at him—and then—and then—oh, Roland, Roland!" for the strong arm was encircling him once more, and Roland was weeping like a child—"when I saw him lie at my feet, and do what I might,

I could not make him stir or breathe, it was hard work not to take that pistol, and follow him. I would have given my own life twice over to have brought back his. I would now, now I have seen you again, old fellow, and your precious wife. You are not jealous of my loving her, are you? For I can tell you I do. Come here, my guardian angel. You do not believe I was a murderer in heart, do you? or that if I had been, I would have come here, even to die?"

His voice failed him; he had become very faint, and Dr. Wartop and Marion had some difficulty in reviving him again. The story of his calamity and subsequent fate, was therefore necessarily delayed; and as the Doctor exhorted quiet, and it was needful to avoid suspicion, the young parents left him for a while, and went up to consult together, and visit their darling.

Mrs. Brudenell was, as usual, at her post; the infant was rarely out of her arms, and her kind face looked weary and worn, from fatigue and sympathising anxiety. She carried the baby into Marion's room, and with doors locked, they talked in whispers of what had happened, and what was yet to do. So much had their full hearts to pour out to each other, that at first there were more tears than words;

but the necessity of deciding on some plan of action, compelled them to self-control, and Marion was beginning to explain her own conduct, when she was stopped by her husband's burst of penitence for his harshness and ingratitude. So bitter was his self-reproach, that all her previous pain was forgotten in the endeavour to put him in charity with himself.

It was easier for her so to do, when she learned that Gervase Wray had overheard a few hurried words, spoken by herself to her uncle, on the day of the *fête*, which had given him the idea that she knew something of the fugitive assassin, and dreaded its coming to her husband's knowledge. The strange pertinacity of the dog had directed and strengthened his suspicions; and he had gone away persuaded that the unfortunate Trail, having thrown himself on her mercy, was being hidden by herself and her friends, till they could secretly arrange his escape. With a shudder Roland remembered how indignantly he had repelled the bare notion of any mercy being shown to the criminal, or any kindness to one who bore his name; and it required all the joy of Harcourt's restoration to enable his brother to bear up under the sense of shame brought by his unhappy deed. Long and anxiously did they consult, for seriously did it behove them to consider what was to be done. For the moment they were tolerably secure: it was known in the household that while the baby's illness continued Dr. Wartop would occupy the private apartments; and sundry hints had been thrown out by Peters of experiments and concoctions he was busy with among the poisons and apparatus always kept there, which would keep the most curious, as she said, from wishing to put their noses in the passage. The rooms occupied by Marion and the child, forming part of the wing Harcourt had built, were immediately over his hiding-place, and quite apart from the rest of the house; and though the first dread lest he had brought the seeds of a contagious disorder with him had been dispelled by his amendment, and that of the infant, the indisposition had been of service in keeping away visitors, and still served as a reason for forbidding the unauthorised intrusion of servants. But this state of things could not last; any hour might bring discovery, and it was necessary to look all the contingencies at once in the face.

Harcourt was alive, and reconciled to him—nothing could quite mar the gladness of that thought; and yet there were many others rising now that might well sadden and perplex the young husband and father. He was no longer master of Morlands, with wealth at command—nay, worse still, he had never been its lawful master; and every farthing he had spent had been in violation of his brother's rights. How was he to stop now, or make restitution, without betraying Harcourt? How, when it should be discovered that he had known of his existence, escape the disgrace of wilfully-committed fraud? His tenants, his servants, his labourers—all were liable to suffer; to what extent he could not yet surmise. He had no right to draw a single cheque, even to pay his housekeeping bills; nothing was really his but the annuity settled on Marion, and the modest sum they had possessed between them when they married. And for Harcourt himself, what could be done? Who could advise him to make open acknowledgment of the truth, when they saw to what he had been driven by the mere dread of its being known? Whether his case were as perilous, under the circumstances, as he believed, Roland could not venture to give an opinion; but he said, and his listeners agreed with him, that the right thing would be to confide in some eminent lawyer, and be guided by his advice. He should talk it over with the Vicar next day, and, if Harcourt did not object, go up to London in the evening; no correspondence would do—it was far too dangerous for anything but a personal interview. Oh, if some step could be devised by which the dear old boy's heart could be set at rest, Roland would care for nothing else—not even if they had all to leave England, and hide themselves with him in the Australian bush.

"We would get old Alexander to bespeak a colonial bishopric for Mr. Brudenell, Minnie, and we would all go off together, and take to sheep-farming. I have a notion you would turn out a capital bushwoman; and Cecil might come out as a missionary, and starve on tea and damper to his heart's content. What would he say if he knew?"

"He would say, tell the truth at all hazards;" said Marion; "and were this his own case, he would do it."

"So would I, but who is to judge for another? We shall know better what to think when he can give us the full particulars."

Late that night, when Roland was taking his turn of watching by the sick-bed, those particulars were given. Harcourt had shrunk from seeing his old friends; he had only endured the necessary presence of doctor and servant, because neither asked him a question upon the past—the one from professional reticence, the other from respect. But to his brother he was yearning to pour out all, and the relief of so doing was the first step towards his recovery.

"Wray told you, of course, how I left him that morning. I did not choose to confess how much money I had fooled away with Lepelletier, but I was resolved to have no more of it, and felt in that mood when nothing but violent exercise would serve my turn. That poor fellow provoked me at starting by sulkiness and dawdling. Roland, I was wrong in his case from first to last; I listened to no advice, and put him in a situation for which he was quite unfit—I humoured him here for my own amusement, and then was savage to find him drunken and disrespectful. I walked off without him, leaving him to follow: Lepelletier heard of my plan, and came after me, bringing poor Bob with him. Of course we played, and, whether he meant it or not, I won every stake, and then wished him good morning. Trail had been drinking most of the time, but as he could take a good deal without betraying himself, I did not notice his manner. When we reached the forester's lodge, where we rested, he wanted to sleep there, and I was resolved to push on. I had a mind to see the Wilde-See; and the more he grumbled, the more determined it made me. My obstinacy, old fellow, as usual, led me wrong—it nearly cost Marion her life, God bless her!—and now it was to cost another in earnest. Roland, do you remember that night, that those two slept here for the first time? I have often wondered since if it were only an old dream for the use of the poet and novelist, that idea of each man having his Fylgia, his tutelary genius, both for evil and good; and whether two such were not then sent to me, for my happiness and my ruin?—Give me some of that stuff of Wartop's—it puts life into a man. He has been good to me, that crusty old fellow—handles me as tenderly as if he were my mother—never seems to remember that I am under a cloud—and yet it is heavy enough, and dark enough, God knows, who only can take it away. . . . Where was I? Going up to the Wilde-See—wild enough, that spot, to please any one. I can see it as I lie here. We had a guide part of the way, and then scrambled on by ourselves; it was evening when we reached the lake, and Trail began to swear at me for bringing him there. He was wet through, he said, with wading through the swampy ground, and he would go no farther for any one. I told him to hold his tongue, and do as he was bid; and the madman cocked my own pistol. I struck him, and he dropped dead. . . . . I do not know how long I was there alone with him, trying to bring him back to life. I know the moon had risen, and was shining on those cold dark waters, when I heard a man's step coming near, and could have blessed him for breaking that worse than solitude. He was a young peasant, a charcoal-burner's son, and, as he let out, in no good odour at home—had got into trouble with the police, and was loose to the ties of society. You wonder at my remembering all this; my dear boy, there is not a single thing that happened that day which I have not gone over in my mind so many times, I have dreaded going mad on the subject, and telling it all to every one who came near. The fellow soon understood my case, and told me it was a bad one; the police would think it a quarrel, and it would go hard with me. I had nearly made up my mind before he came. I was guilty of blood—no matter how—and I shrank, I cannot describe with what abject terror, from the scenes I must go through if I gave myself up. Better I had died by his hand than he by mine; better I should die to you all, than bring disgrace on my father's name, on my own, and on yours. With the help of the youth, I went through it all; we took off the poor fellow's clothes, tenderly enough, and wrapped him in my plaid, and buried him under a pile of logs, which the forester lighted. I changed my dress for his, putting my own into a bundle: you wonder at my nerve, perhaps; but I was turned to stone, and felt none of those smaller tortures at the time. I rewarded my friend liberally, and he told me he should escape at once, and go to America. Then I walked on to Wildbad; showed myself at the hotel, and in several shops, where I acted my part as if it were on the stage, talking broken German, and announcing the speedy arrival of my master. At one or two other places I took care to leave the same report; I think I had some of the cunning of madness upon me at that time; and after that, I put on my own dress, and struck across France. I had money, and passports, and brains for emergencies, and wore several disguises before I quite baffled pursuit. I wished you to believe me dead, and meant never to be heard of again.

"I cannot describe the state of my mind through all this; but if a man can be insane without losing his faculties, I was. I lived and moved in a dream of horror, in which I seemed to be isolated from the rest of mankind, and compelled to pass existence alone. I had sufficient strength left to refrain from brandy—the very smell of it reminded me of my long efforts by the lake, rubbing it into the dead man's temple, trying to force it between his teeth. Oh, when shall I ever forget that night? Thank you, dear fellow—just a mouthful—your wife makes lemonade like Miss Nightingale, and it does me more good than if it were made by any one else.

"I was wandering one day through a village in the south of France, when I fell in with some Zouaves, and they proposed I should enlist. I passed myself as an American, and they told me they had all nations in their corps. People used to talk in the Crimean war of Eton men being found among them; I cannot say I discovered any. They were eager for recruits, and asked no questions about my antecedents. I enlisted, and went with the regiment to Algeria. It would make a couple of good volumes if I wrote down my two years' experience under the Imperial eagles; but a sick heart makes a poor hero. I was still in my dream-land of penance, and went through drudgery and drill as I had gone through everything else, from that hour at the Wilde-See. An officer took a fancy to me, for curing his horse when it was ill, and made me his servant. There was retribution in that, and it suited me. I learned to polish boots to a nicety —don't, dear fellow, don't"—as Roland's sobs broke in on the narrative; "it was not much worse than fagging; don't be unhappy about that. The work, the rations, the position, were nothing to the dull, gnawing pain at the heart —the slow fire in the brain.

"That came to a crisis at last; cholera and dysentery carried off some files of our men, and I was ill in my turn, and lay for hours quiet in hospital, and by degrees began to come to myself, like the son in the parable. I used to think of you and Marion, and of Brudenell, and Percival, till I could imagine I heard you all in church—who knows? Perhaps I did, if what some believe be true. I found many things true at last, which I had doubted before . . . . . . is that the Doctor coming, to make me hold my tongue? Don't let him in just yet. To lie here, and tell you everything like this, is worth all his potions, and you may let him know as much.

"I got up at last, but the surgeon pronounced me unfit for service; lungs out of order, or something, and I had my discharge, and a passage to Marseilles. A sick soldier is always a pet among the people there, and wherever I went, I was kindly treated. I roughed it, of course, but that I was used to; and in time I reached Paris. It was at a cheap *restaurant* there that I met with Lepelletier, down on his luck, and studying economy till he had replenished his purse. I could disguise myself from everybody else, but not from that fellow; and he had been watching me some time before I was aware. I affected not to know him, and gave him the slip, in spite of his attempts to dog me; but I read mischief in his eyes, and knew that he remembered his breakfast at Gernsbach. I was, by this time, nearly done for, and felt I must see you again before I died. I had promised Marion I would not meet her till I could do so as a brother should; what a brother I had proved myself!—and yet, I did long for one kind look from those dear eyes of hers, as much as to feel your hand in mine again, old boy. Rather a difference in our muscles now; I should think twice before I attempted to hold in a pair of young horses of your training. Have you got the greys back, by the way?"

"Was it likely?" asked Roland, reproachfully.

"Well, I did not know; it was all my pride that made me part with them, because you could manage them, and I could not. I crossed the Channel, and walked here in what sort of dress you may imagine; I changed my ragged regimentals for some slops at Calais. I had not much fear of recognition, only of not holding out long enough. I arrived here late, and I was loitering along the road, for when it came to the point, my heart began to fail; and I saw Lepelletier coming to meet me. I guessed where he had been, and had just time to get out of his sight. I hid myself in the park till I thought every one would be in bed, meaning then to try and let myself in by my private key, which I had taken abroad with me, and never parted with. How I had longed to be in here once more, if only to die in peace!—and yet I hesitated up to the last moment. I did not know but that you might have altered the rooms, or that the door might be bolted, and I should not be able to get in, and perhaps alarm the house. I ventured at last, and found myself face to face with Marion. How lovely she looked! I had seen nothing so sweet and good for so long, and felt so unworthy to touch even the hem of her dress, that between my shame and her terror, it was some little time before we could speak to each other. I am afraid I gave her a very severe shock, for when I was kneeling by her, and took her hands in mine, they were as cold as marble. I had to attend to her first, God bless her! but her turn soon came. As soon as she recovered herself, and understood how I came to be there, I had found a sister indeed. She was afraid to call even Peters, but she went herself, and fetched me food and coffee, and made my bed, and brought me all the comforts that had become forgotten luxuries, and never left me till she had done all a woman could do to keep my body and soul from sinking. We agreed that the Brudenells must be told; I only begged them not to come near me: till I knew whether you would receive me or not, I could not bear to be seen even by them. And here I have been ever since, and very ill I was at first; it has been terribly hot, and I was in such a high fever the other night, they had to send for Wartop. He says I may live yet; the question is, if I do, what is to be done next?"

"Noll, you know one thing—you are master here."

"Master? not I. I have abdicated to William and Mary, and I am not come back as a Pretender."

Roland shook his head, but would not agitate him by continuing on the subject. Exhausted with so much talking, Harcourt soon after fell asleep, and his brother watched by him till morning.

With the morning came an unexpected trouble, though one which it would not have been unreasonable to expect. Marion was ill—it was hoped only from fatigue and anxiety, but her state was such that it was absolutely necessary the baby should be removed, and Mrs. Brudenell was to take it to the Vicarage, and find it a nurse among her village friends. It was a heavy trial to both aunt and niece, but Dr. Wartop was imperative, and the young mother's fears for her little one's safety gave her courage to bear the separation, and the loss of Mrs. Brudenell's tender care. Neither owned to the other the thought uppermost in their minds—that if this illness had been brought in by the fugitive, it might prove serious. They spoke bravely at parting, and more bravely still to poor Roland, who needed all the comfort that could be given him, deprived of his wife's support just when he needed it most. He was a devoted nurse, and never left her except when he was required by Harcourt, to whom he had to carry as cheerful accounts as he could, in order to calm his anguish.

"I have brought a curse with me, and it falls on the innocent," was constantly on his lips, and again and again he would implore Roland's forgiveness, revealing more of his undying attachment to Marion than he knew, but in such a form that it excited compassionate indulgence, and not jealousy. The comfort of the Vicar's presence was denied to them both by the fear of carrying infection to the infant, and when Roland suggested confiding in Cecil, Harcourt shrank from the mention of his name.

"I will see no one—neither Percival nor Wray, nor even Stella. Let me but pick up strength enough to travel, and I will set you free, and none of you shall suffer another pang on my account," was his answer—so bitterly spoken, that his brother could say no more. It was Dr. Wartop whose blunt sense opened the fugitive's eyes to the true state of the predicament in which they were all placed.

"It is very well for you, sir, to sit there, and say you have abandoned your rights, and so forth; do you think honest people, like your brother and sister, will ever profit by such an extraordinary complication of circumstances? I know them both, and though for your safety's sake they go on now because they cannot help it, yet as soon as it is possible, they will be striking tent, and starting somewhere, to live on the means, whatever that may be, that they can conscientiously call their own. Roland has been talking it over with me, and I know Mrs. Clarendon's mind was made up from the very first. A report has got about, somehow, that they are in difficulties, and it is said that it is owing to some connexion of your sister's—and when I saw the Squire the other day at Durningham, he began to sound me on the subject, so I rather encouraged the notion. It is perfectly true, and may make your brother's future course somewhat easier."

The consequence of this speech was, that when Harcourt next saw Roland, he urgently besought him, as soon as Marion could safely be left, to go up to London as they had agreed, lay the whole case before a first-rate lawyer, and bring him back with him to Morlands. It was becoming urgent that some such step should be taken, for another whisper had begun to circulate—how it had arisen no one knew—that there was some mystery connected with Dr. Wartop's residence in the private apartments; the word "insanity" had been dropped, and there was no knowing to what such a rumour might grow. So when Marion was out of danger, and only the weakness left, for which the Doctor's care and Peters's watching could be trusted to provide, Roland reluctantly started on his anxious journey. Percival found out he was going, and met him at the station.

"I have no fears—you may shake hands with me," he said, as Clarendon was drawing back; "I have a theory of my own about infection, though I cannot explain it to you now; and I trust all that fear is over now, as your wife is better."

"She is better—or I should not be here."

"You know how it was she came to that poor woman's death-bed—I fear it was too much for her, but what could I do?"

"You did right, perfectly right," said Roland, turning pale. "I did not know she was dead."

"She died that evening. I buried her at Durningham, as she desired."

"Thank you, Cecil: you are the best fellow that ever lived. I was very hard and cruel about that woman, but Marion did her duty, as she always does; and you helped her. I cannot stay to talk—I must go——"

"Something is the matter, or you would not leave her, I am sure."

"I am obliged to go up on urgent business—it has been delayed too long already. You will be at hand, Cecil, old fellow, if she should send for you?"

"Depend upon me. Roland, may I ask this

—is it true what people say—that you are in difficulties?"

"In difficulties? I should think I was. I shall probably have to leave Morlands, and work for my wife and child. No great grievance either, you will say."

"I do say it. More—I am glad to hear it. You will be a happier man, and I trust a blessing will rest upon you, which you could never have here. If only I might share it!"

"You, Cecil? so good and earnest as you are?"

But Cecil had turned away, and the train came up before another word was spoken.

CHAPTER XI.

MARION'S DREAM.

"AND Roland is gone, with his wife still confined to her bed? It must be urgent business indeed. And he told you himself he was in difficulties, poor fellow? I wonder how that can be, with his noble income. Is it possible that Marion could have been entangled in any of Mr. Saville's affairs?"

"It may be so," said Cecil; "I cannot tell."

He was sitting in the cool of the evening, by Stella's side, at the open window of the White House, with no sound near but those sweet rural murmurs, which are more soothing than silence; and though he had come in, intending only to stay half an hour, the longer he sat there, the more difficult he found it to depart. Her mother was taking her usual nap on the sofa, and Stella had never seemed so gentle, so accessible, since he had allowed her to feel that his happiness depended on her smile. She was sadder than was her usual wont, and if ever there is a time and season when sadness craves the relief of outpouring, and pride and reserve melt before sympathy, it is in the twilight of such an evening as this was.

"I am very sorry for Roland," Stella observed, after an interval of thoughtfulness; "I envied those two their lot a little while ago, but they are no happier than others, after all."

"You envied them, you say? Not their fortune, I am sure; you have too noble a spirit to covet money, or money's worth. What you did envy was the love that gave value to the rest, and which might have been yours, in that very home."

"You are not to think that," she said, without appearing offended; "now that all is past and gone, I may frankly speak of it—I believe I misled others as well as myself—but there was never anything between me and my poor cousin beyond cousinly intimacy and preference. Nor, on looking back dispassionately on what I felt for him—sadly as I have mourned his loss—do I believe there ever would have been."

"Dare I believe you, Miss Porchester?"

"It will need some courage, and when you do believe, some charity. All I really cared for, was the gratification of my pride and ambition; and if I had married him, I should not have made him happy."

The tears were in her eyes, and her tone was sincere and humble. Percival sat some minutes without making any reply.

"I am over-bold in my questions," he said at last, "but as your friend, I cannot help asking—is your present choice one to make *you* happy?"

She hid her face for a moment, then lifting it with sudden energy—"Happy I cannot say, in such a world as this—but that it would make me better, wiser, holier, that I am certain."

"Holier, with a man like Gervase Wray?"

She smiled in scorn through her tears, and as he looked in her face in the moonlight, he thought it was more beautiful than ever.

"Of Gervase Wray, whether he cares for me or not, I have learned lately what would break my heart if I loved him; as it is, we shall not quarrel, but I can never think of him again as a friend."

She did not explain why, and he did not

ask. His heart was throbbing so painfully as almost to take away his breath.

"You have made a choice, and it is neither of those. Oh, Stella, Stella, if I were but less unworthy, I might hazard all, and grasp at a shadow of hope—but it comes too late for one who has fallen so grievously as I."

"Too late?" The words and the tone chilled Miss Porchester's heart; she trembled at what she had done, and could neither speak nor move. He took her hand and pressed it to his lips.

"Tell me, Stella, if you knew I had done wrong, and still durst not confess it, could you forgive me? Could you trust me again?"

She struggled to answer calmly, but she was choking with tears.

"I do not know—I cannot tell—it must depend on what you felt for me. You frighten me with your mysterious hints. If your conscience has so much to bear, what do you suppose has mine, who never, since I was a woman, had a thought of what was right, till you put it into my head? If I ever have a hope of being a shade better, which is only now and then, it will be to you I shall owe it; and to shake my faith in you now, would be a bad business indeed."

He paused awhile, then whispered softly, "Should you be afraid of the night air? Would it hurt you to take a turn in the garden?"

"That I cannot tell unless I try."

They stepped out accordingly, and wandered along the gravel paths, a delicious breeze playing round their temples, laden with the sweets of the flowering shrubs around them. And there he confided to her his secret, and placed his fate in her hands—his one chance of happiness at her mercy.

How she received his confidence, how she used her mercy, startling and bewildering as his revelation was, may be inferred from the length of time the interview lasted. There was a great deal to talk over—much that was of serious import, and the dark masses of the Morlands woods lay full in her view the while; but the more they talked, the less easy it became to go back to the house. So there they lingered, longer than was prudent—but who was to remind them of prudence then? Prudence, had she begun to interfere at all, would have had too much to do, to think of dews and exhalations; and would probably have been as much heeded in the one case as in the other. Never were two people apparently less suited—never were prospects less free from obstructions and hindrances—but before they parted that night, they were pledged to each other heart and hand.

Late as it was when Cecil at last took leave, he felt too excited for rest, and wandered slowly through the park, musing on what he had done, as if in a happy dream from which he feared to wake, till he found himself at the little gate leading into the pleasure-ground. As he stopped to consider whether to pass through or go round, he thought he smelt burning, and moving a little farther, where the house could be seen, was horror-stricken to perceive a cloud of smoke and tongues of flame issuing from the upper windows. In a few minutes he had reached the entrance, and was ringing violently at the bell; then rushed to the stable-yard, where his shouts speedily roused the old watch-dog, whose barks seconded his efforts to waken the sleepers within. Strange how soundly people will sleep at times, when their lives hang on a thread! It seemed to Cecil as if he should never make himself heard; but at last windows and doors opened, and heads were thrust out in alarm, and at the cry of "Fire!" female voices uttered responsive shrieks of dismay. Percival pressed forward as soon as he could obtain admittance, and made his way to the foot of the large oaken staircase. The smoke was thickening fast, and he stumbled in the darkness on something lying prone on the floor—a woman's form, too heavy for him to lift. His shouts brought helpers to his side, and poor Mrs. Peters was raised with difficulty, and carried, still insensible, into the air. Her dress was singed and disordered, and it struck them all at once, that she must have fled down stairs to escape the fire, and in her terror had fallen and stunned herself. If so, what had become of her mistress?

"Merciful Heaven protect her! Run and rouse up the Doctor, wherever he is, and let him see what he can do for the woman; and you, Bowles, Richards, all who have any pluck among you, come and help me save Mrs. Clarendon!"

There was no flinching on the part of the men—they were ready to do anything; but who could penetrate a wall of smoke, that stifled them as they tried to ascend? Cecil dashed up half way—his weak lungs failing almost immediately, he was carried back again by Bowles, to renew the attempt as soon as he regained his breath, and only to be beaten down as before. The smoke rolled along the gallery like the waves of the sea, and the roaring of flames was enough to strike terror into the boldest heart.

"The back-stairs, let us try them!" cried Richards, and they rushed in that direction; but, alas! those stairs did not communicate with the end of the house where the fire was raging; the enemy was still between them and the victim they were endeavouring to rescue. "Ladders! ladders!" was the cry, as once more they retraced their steps, and hurried out into the grounds, where a crowd was now fast gathering from the village, roused by the ringing of the alarm-bell from the stables. Engines were expected every minute, and many hands were employed in carrying out the furniture and paintings from the lower rooms, as the dryness of the weather had made everything like tinder, and fears were entertained that the whole house would be consumed before effectual means could be taken. But what would Roland reck of house or property if his heart's best treasure were not rescued too? and oh! how long it seemed before a ladder could be found!

"They've brought one now, Mr. Percival—here it comes, thank God!" almost sobbed Bowles, as a party of labourers dragged in the desired instrument of safety; "we'll save her now, or die for it, that we will. Oh, sir, sir——" clutching Cecil's coat in sudden terror, such as no danger had roused in his stout heart, "look there—who, and what is *that?*"

Marion had slept, the first part of the night, the quiet sleep of languid convalescence. She had wished to be left alone, without a light; and at her desire, Dr. Wartop had gone to bed, and Peters to lie down in another room. Gradually the invalid became aware, even in her sleep, of something oppressive to her breathing: it mingled with her dreams, and brought back, as has happened to more than one of us at times, the recollection of another dream, long ago passed away. Again she heard the roar of waters, and the shouts of men calling to her to escape, and as before, could not move hand or foot, and panting, struggling, woke up at last, to find her room full of smoke, making her weak eyes smart painfully, and filling her lungs with the choking fumes of burnt wood. She made a faint effort to ring the bell, and started to feel the wall hot to her touch. She shrieked to Peters to come to her, but no one answered; she tried to creep from her bed, but a deadly faintness seized her, and she sank back on her pillow. The smoke grew thicker and thicker, and she knew what it must mean—fire was close at hand, and she could not escape; she was already nearly exhausted with the difficulty of breathing.

She thought—as in the most tremendous moments the mind has power to think—of all she had to leave—of her husband, her child, her uncle and aunt, her unhappy brother, her friends and her poor, and felt that such a death was bitter indeed. Strangely, vividly, came back before her mental vision the happiest scenes of her short life; she was watching the Jungfrau in the moonlight, with Roland by her side—she was listening to his tender vows in her uncle's study—she was sharing his embrace with his new-born child. And all to end like this! Who would tell him when he returned? How would he ever know how dearly she had loved him?

But even in that agony of the shadow of death, her faith stood by her like a strengthening angel. If it were His will, in whom she trusted, helpless in His hands, she could look up, and trust Him still. He could deliver, or He could help her to bear the worst, and He could comfort them all when she was gone. A prayer for blessings on her beloved, for pardon and mercy for herself, was on her lips as she lay with tightly-clasped hands, and shortening breath, waiting for her doom, when the door opened for a moment, giving her one glimpse of flashing flame beyond, and, as it closed again, Harcourt sprang to her bedside.

"My Marion! thank God I have reached you! Do not be frightened, we have time enough. You can trust your brother to take care of you."

He flung the shutters and window open to let out the smoke, and the moonbeams shone quietly in, strangely contrasted with the scene they looked upon. The air revived Marion a little, and she half raised herself on her elbow.

"Is it you, Harcourt? I thought no one could come near me, and that I was left to die."

"I thought so too, and it gave me strength to come. They are getting a ladder, so we have plenty of time; do not be afraid." He was stripping a blanket from the bed to wrap round her. "Can you walk, dear Marion? for if not, you must trust yourself to my arms again. I carried you in, and I can well carry you out."

"I tried to stand just now, but could not. No, Harcourt, you are too weak to lift me; you cannot save me alone—save yourself to comfort Roland, and tell him—tell him——"

"Hush—do not agitate yourself more than

you can help. We can but try, and if we fail, we will leave the world together."

He laid the blanket down, and stooped over her. " It is your brother, remember, Marion —only your brother. Trust him, and pray for him, that he may be allowed to save, or die with you."

She put her weak arms round his neck, and kissed him for the first time; then passively allowed him to wrap her from head to foot, and lift her in his arms. He tried the passage first, as it was not easy to reach the parapet below the window; but the fire was gaining ground too rapidly—it had already seized on the walls of the room, and the paper was blistering in all directions. With great difficulty he let himself down with his helpless burden upon the parapet, and looked below. What were they all about there that they brought no ladder, and the very stone-work growing hot under his feet? Ha! there was one coming; and there, too, was a man who had sense and courage—and he lifted his voice like a trumpet, and called Cecil Percival by name.

And the up-turned faces saw by the blended light of fire and moon the master they had mourned as dead.

Percival heard the voice, and knew the

form, and while every one else recoiled with fear, or was stupified with amazement, rushed forwards to respond to his appeal, planted the ladder which the men were nearly letting fall, and mounted to meet him half way. By their united efforts, Marion was carried down, and all three were safe on the terrace before any of the spectators had recovered from the shock of the surprise. Cecil's voice soon brought assistance round them, and busy hands took possession of poor Marion, enveloping her in coats and shawls, till a mattress was procured, on which she was borne, at Percival's desire, to the White House. He would have walked by her side, but he could not leave Harcourt, whose energy had expended itself in that brave deed, and who was now leaning on his shoulder for support, with a wild light in his eyes, more like joy than had been seen there for many a weary day.

"Let the walls burn down!" he said, as curious and wondering faces came round, to see if it were really himself, and not a spectre or illusion. "The jewel is safe, and no matter for the box and the cotton. Ay, my good fellows, you may stare as you please now—it is no longer a secret that I am alive, and I do not care who knows it. Bear me witness, all of you, that I have paid my debt sevenfold—

a life like *hers* for one like *his*—is not that compensation enough? If not, I have nothing more worth giving; certainly not my own. I say, Percival, help me to bed, will you, somewhere—for I want to hold out till Roland comes back, for his sake and hers."

His head drooped with the words, and Percival, the tears running down his cheeks, carried him, with the help of Bowles, to the house of Mrs. Porchester.

The engines had now arrived, and strenuous efforts were being made to save the remainder of the mansion, but with that he had no more concern; he could only think of the lives that had been saved, and thank God in his heart that he had spoken the truth to Stella.

"Is that you, Roland?"

"Yes, dear old fellow—are you better now?"

"I suppose so, as I can talk about it. I have been lying here some time wondering whether I were alive or dead, or out of my senses. Have I been talking in my sleep?"

"No, and you are not to talk much now. You are to get strong by degrees, and live to make us all happy."

"I see. Get me some water, dear boy.

Thanks—I begin to remember. Is Morlands done for?"

"Only that wing—no lives lost, thank Heaven, and—and——" here Roland's hands closed on his brother's, "thank you, too, Noll. I must not say what I feel now."

"No, don't, for I could not bear it. The darling! She was sensible the whole time, and lay in my arms like a trusting child. Once my foot nearly slipped, and I felt her shiver, but she only murmured a prayer. I could have died then very happily—now it will be hard, weary work to go, and there is a great deal to be done first. Have you secured advice?"

"All right; Mr. —— will be down to-morrow. They telegraphed for me, and I left word that he might follow."

"Then I must keep quiet to-day, and be ready for him. I should like to see Stella once more—and then I want to speak to dear old Brudenell."

Stella was close at hand, longing, yet almost dreading to be admitted; and when Roland brought her to the bedside, her emotion at the sight of Harcourt's altered features would hardly allow her to speak. He held her by the hand, and gazed at her wistfully and admiringly; for it was new to him to see her thus, and it gave her face the gentleness he had sometimes felt to be the attraction it wanted. He gazed, but it was as we gaze at something that reminds us of scenes long past, the memory of which is pleasant, but it is a memory, and nothing more. He had little to say to her, beyond asking her forgiveness, not only for the shame he had brought on all his kindred, but for any unkindness or neglect of which he might have been guilty; and then he spoke of Cecil Percival, and saw by her blush how matters stood. She knelt by his pillow, and told him the truth, and how she had trifled with them both, and had found happiness when she expected it least; and that the devotion of the rest of her life would be all too little to make her worthy of the attachment of such a man. And when he asked if he could do anything to promote her happiness, she owned with tears there was one thing troubled her sadly—not the want of fortune—Cecil knew all her affairs, and they were both prepared to face poverty and privation—she should mind nothing if she could but see him easy in his mind; he was quite ill with nervous self-reproach; she might not explain the cause—and all she implored her cousins was to deal with him tenderly, and give him comfort.

"Is it connected with my wretched story? I see it is," said Harcourt, rousing himself from his lethargy "I have brought misery everywhere—let me remedy it while I can. Go to him, Roland—go this moment. Learn the whole truth, and recollect you owe your darling's life more to him than to me. He did his best to save us—it is the work he has been doing all along."

Roland was not sorry to withdraw, for his own excited feelings were fast overpowering the self-control he had been forced to exercise before his brother. He went to the room where his friends were waiting to confer with him; the Vicar he had seen already, for he met him at the station, but he was not quite prepared to find both the Percivals, and the General and his daughter, and to be assailed by all in turn, Cecil only excepted, with eager questions as to what they could severally or collectively do to help him. All knew the terrible inference that must be drawn from the fact of Harcourt's existence, though no one could put the question of his guilt or innocence in plain words—and Roland could say little to satisfy them. Harcourt alone could answer, and he must not be disturbed. There was one person, however, whom he must thank before them all for his gallant exertions to save his dear wife, and that was Cecil—and pressing through the others to where the curate stood, he wrung his hand with a vigour that would at any other time have given him pain, but was then hardly felt. With a flush on his brow, and a sad humility in his whole bearing, that almost transformed him into another man, Cecil turned from his friend to those whose murmur of applause was seconding his gratitude.

"Before you honour me with your good opinion," he said, slowly and firmly, "I beg you will hear what I have to say. I am not the truthful man some of you have believed me to be—I have been guilty for two years of carrying on a deception, which may be palliated by the circumstances, but cannot be excused. I make no excuse—I only state the fact. When that poor body was found by the Wilde-See, and brought to Baden for identification, I was the only person who could attempt to do so. I told the authorities it was too late—it could not be identified then; I told a lie—I knew it was the body of Robert Trail."

"You did?" said Roland, unable to believe his senses.

"Yes; not by the face—no one could tell

that—it was by a mark on his arm that I remembered perfectly, having often seen it when he was ill at Durningham—a device tattooed just below the elbow. The arms and hands were in tolerable preservation. I could have sworn to that arm—and I held my peace."

"What made you do so?" asked the General.

"I knew exactly how the case must stand—that if Trail were dead, and Harcourt had escaped in his clothes, Harcourt must have killed him. I could not betray his secret—I could not! I believe, were it to happen again, I should do as I then did; and yet I know I was wrong, for it was untruth, and want of faith. I thought more of what others would suffer by the knowledge than of what was simply right, and I have suffered quite enough in my conscience since to convince me, if I needed convincing. If Roland can forgive me—perhaps my uncle will—who has had a great deal to put up with from my pride and presumption. If they cannot—I can only say it is just."

"I could not have believed," said Mr. Brudenell to his wife, when describing the scene to her afterwards, "that any one could have been so changed by any circumstance in so short a time, as this has changed Cecil Percival. He disarmed us all; there was no one who could have breathed a word against him, even when he left the room. There was a dignity in his self-abasement, that made us feel little in our own eyes. And yet he was quite right—it would have been wiser, as well as better, if he had spoken the truth at the first. Harcourt might have been spared much that he has suffered; and Roland all that he is suffering now. Unless I am much mistaken, and Wartop too, there is more sorrow in store for him yet."

They were not mistaken; the sorrow came on even faster than they had looked for it. The foreboding that had driven Clarendon back to his home—without which, indeed, he would never have returned—was only too swiftly to be fulfilled; and from that night that he rescued his sister, Harcourt's strength sank rapidly, defying medical skill and tender nursing. He roused himself for a long interview with the experienced lawyer his brother had engaged, and under his instructions secured Roland and his tenants, as far as possible, from inconvenience; and in the presence of the Vicar, and of Mr. Percival of Durningham, dictated a full confession of his sorely-repented act of manslaughter—asking pardon of God and man, and leaving it to his brother to make what poor atonement money could make, to the memory of the dead, and any survivor to whom his rights descended.

When all this was done, he seemed to have laid his earthly cares aside, and Mr. Brudenell had no difficulty now in winning his ear to listen to the truth. Misfortune had been a teacher from whom he could not shrink, and her lessons had prepared him for those of his old friend, who never left him, night or day. Of his other friends he took leave with affectionate tenderness, as if relinquishing his hold on them and on the world; but to Mr. Brudenell, and his brother and sister, he clung to the last. Marion was too weak herself to be his nurse, but she persisted in creeping down to his room, and however restless he might have been before, he was soothed the moment he heard her step. He never spoke to her of the past, or recalled his old passionate love—but his eyes dwelt on her when they could dwell on nothing else, and her name was on his lips when he died.

Faithful to his last charge, Roland did his utmost to find a representative of the unfortunate Trail, and, with Cecil's help, did at last discover a not undeserving family of orphans, on whom he could relieve himself by pouring out his bounty. Another piece of tardy justice was also done, by the removal of the inscription in the cemetery of Baden, and the substitution of another, explaining the mournful truth. It was read by the good Abbé, who remembered the funeral, and the grief of the English stranger, and understood at last the words that had so interested him then, and why that grief had been so exceedingly bitter.

Percival was slow in recovering his strength and spirits, but his uncle's fatherly kindness stood him in good stead; he settled on him a liberal allowance; promoted, with Roland's co-operation, his marriage with Miss Porchester, and sent them abroad, with the promise, that if he returned fit for work, he should come back to Durningham, where Mr. Holmby was ready to receive him with open arms. Roland, at Marion's special request, not only insisted on making a settlement on Stella, but helped her and her mother out of all their difficulties; and so sorely had the young lady felt their burden, that she made a wise resolve never to assume such another. She married Cecil in the autumn, went with him on a pleasant tour alone, and has since settled down at Durningham with as much good will as if she were actually the Lady of the Manor, which she fully intends to be some day.

Gervase Wray also went abroad, and remained there. The breach between them was never quite explained, but those who indulged in gossip, surmised that Mrs. Jones knew more than most people on that subject—she having received a private budget of letters and papers, reflecting so little credit on Mr. Wray's past, and suggesting so little comfort for his future, that a less high-spirited individual than Stella would have been deterred from sharing it. He was a man with whom any one could be friendly, so long as they only saw the surface; once go deeper, and friendship, such as deserves the name, was morally impossible.

Roland and Marion have several children now, and Morlands has repaired its injuries, and its galleries echo with little feet, and its gardens with little voices. And the Vicar, as his step grows slower, and his eyesight more dim, on his path to his quiet rest, finds a never-failing joy in those tiny fingers that cling to his, as if they knew his value, and would detain him if they could. They cannot do it long, but they make him very happy, and their own happiness in his presence is not shadowed, like that of their parents, with the dread of the parting that is to come. Roland

and Marion are devoted to those tried friends, who have been to them as second parents; and Mrs. Brudenell's yearning heart has vacancies no longer, for Marion's children are to her as her own. She has her full share of their love, and of the care and anxiety from which, in this world, love is never free.

It was long before any of them could speak of him they had lost without tears—it will be longer still before they forget him. The heir of Morlands bears his name; and when Marion bends over his pillow at night, the blessings that are so tenderly breathed on the living Harcourt, often blend with those that keep sacred the memory of the dead.

THE END.

CPSIA information can be obtained
at www.ICGtesting.com
Printed in the USA
LVHW100514130422
716029LV00002B/105

9 783752 589832